TYRELL'S GUNS

When Sam Tyrell arrives in the valley, it's with the intention of expanding the boundaries of the Circle T ranch, and he won't let anyone prevent him from his course. And, as everyone knows, he won't hesitate to use gunfire to get his way. Then one man steps into the breach. Hank Carty boldly opposes Tyrell's plans — he's determined to stand his ground. Is he brave or simply foolish? Only the final showdown in the valley will tell . . .

BEN COADY

TYRELL'S GUNS

Complete and Unabridged

LINFORD
Leicester

First published in Great Britain in 2011 by
Robert Hale Limited
London

First Linford Edition
published 2012
by arrangement with
Robert Hale Limited
London

British Library CIP Data

Coady, Ben.
    Tyrell's guns.- -(Linford western library)
    1. Western stories.
    2. Large type books.
    I. Title II. Series
    823.9'2–dc23

    ISBN 978–1–4448–1092–9

Published by
F. A. Thorpe (Publishing)
Anstey, Leicestershire

Set by Words & Graphics Ltd.
Anstey, Leicestershire
Printed and bound in Great Britain by
T. J. International Ltd., Padstow, Cornwall

This book is printed on acid-free paper

1

'Tyrell!'

Hank Carty's angry yell at the man bellied up to the bar of the Broken Arrow saloon, basking in the company of most of the saloon's imbibers who had gathered round to partake greedily of the free liquor on offer, caused a noticeable dip in the man's popularity as the freeloaders drifted away.

Sam Tyrell's contemptuous snort told them that they weren't fooling anyone but themselves.

The saddle-hardened man put the one shot glass back on the highly polished bartop and turned slowly, his grin becoming more and more mocking of Carty. His curiously shaped eyebrow, which gave his left eye an odd angle relative to his right, was raised quizzically. Two of Tyrell's hardcases stepped forward, one on either side of their boss, whose walnut gun butts were polished from frequent use. The pistols were low-slung and thonged. Jack Almont and Henry Scranton were typical of the coterie of gun-handy *hombres* with whom Tyrell had surrounded himself in the months since he had arrived to establish the Circle T in the valley south of Lucky Hollow. It was a ranch that had constantly expanded its boundaries, and seemed set to swallow up the entire valley. Almont and Scranton were two of New Mexico's gun-handiest fellas and formed the backbone of the Tyrell outfit, who made life hellish for those who opposed his steady march to complete dominance of all things in valley and town. Tyrell had cleverly used carrot and stick: carrot for the town, where he had greased palms and used largesse to smooth his path, so that by now most townsfolk were beholden to him in one form or another. Some of them were of high standing, some were relatively insignificant, but none was in a position to raise a voice against Tyrell's shenanigans in the valley. That had fallen to the feisty Hank Carty. And the stick Tyrell wielded in the valley, where gun and boot were employed against anyone who refused Tyrell's paltry offer to sell up and move on.

'Pa, you'll buck Tyrell too much,' Lucy Carty had more than once cautioned her father. 'Is the valley worth dying for?'

'I guess, for me, it is,' had been his often stated position.

Jack Almont's answer to the problem was simple: shoot or hang Carty. It was not a view that Tyrell was averse to, but he'd been holding off, ignoring warnings about those ranchers left getting backbone from Carty, because of Lucy Carty and his hankering to make her his woman.

'Some mornin' you'll wake up and there'll be a lynch mob on your doorstep,' Almont had warned Tyrell. 'If you want Carty's daughter, just ride over there and take her. Right now you can do anything you want in this neck of the woods. So don't risk losin' your grip, boss, that's what I say. Carty's a real rouser of men,' Almont had cautioned. Of course Tyrell saw the sense of his hireling's utterances, but at this juncture the heat of his hankering outweighed the sound logic of Jack Almont's good sense.

'Carty.' Tyrell intoned his challenger's name scornfully. 'And this was such a nice morning, fellas.' His hired enforcers sniggered.

'Don't matter much what kinda day a man dies on, Mr Tyrell,' Almont said, his hands dropping to the butts of the double rig he wore.

Hank Carty eyed Almont with pure contempt. 'Cow-dung like you don't scare me none, Almont,' he growled.

Sam Tyrell grabbed Almont's right wrist, held it firmly in his grasp, and with it Almont's six-gun in its holster.

'That wasn't a nice thing to say, Carty,' Tyrell said. 'It's the kind of thing that a maddened man might react to, don't you reckon?'

4

Hank Carty said, uncompromisingly, 'The truth can be as hard as gall to swallow.'

Sam Tyrell let loose a long sigh and leaned an elbow on the bar. 'You know, Carty, you seem to be a man with a hankering to hurry up the hereafter.'

'How's that pretty daughter of yours this fine day, Carty?' Henry Scranton's laughter was goading. 'Since I first set eyes on her when I come to work for Mr Tyrell a coupla months back, that filly's sure given me some real breath-stealin' dreams.'

'Shuddup!' Tyrell barked.

'Sure am sorry, boss,' Scranton said. 'But you can't blame a man for dreamin', now can ya?' Put down, Scranton's mood was meaner than it had been, and that was pretty mean to start with. 'Bet I could make her feel real good in herself, Mr Carty. If you took off that tight leash you've got her on. She gimme the look a coupla times our paths crossed. So I figure that if it comes down to any hanky-panky with

Carty's daughter,' his dark narrow eyes bore into Tyrell, 'I got first call.'

Almont could see Tyrell's anger rise to unstoppable. He knew that in his present mood Scranton would not hesitate to pick up any gauntlet that Tyrell might foolishly throw down. He had plans far beyond mere wages for the next couple of months that it would take for Tyrell to own every blade of grass in the valley and every soul in town; he had a scheme where he saw himself fitting in well into the future. Almont wasn't then aware that Scranton was thinking along the same lines.

'You figure that a nice young lady such as Lucy Carty would have anything to do with a fella who's sampled Mex whorehouse trash, Henry?' Almont snorted.

'Never knowed a woman with her skirt up who was choosy,' Scranton sneered.

Hank Carty's fist shot out and landed with full force on Scranton's jaw. The gunnie tumbled back across the saloon, going down heavily when his legs got tangled with his efforts to remain upright. He hit the floor, then came up fast, six-gun cocked, fighting mad. 'Hope ya've got that lucky Yankee silver in your shirt pocket, Carty.'

The silver dollar Scranton referred to was Hank Carty's lucky piece, and rightly so named. It had a dent in its centre that had stopped a Reb bullet on the last day of the Civil War. Carty was caught cold, looking down the barrel of a six-gun, only seconds away from oblivion, and thinking that his rash action would leave his much loved daughter at the mercy of men like Scranton. In the wild territory of New Mexico there were plenty of men like Scranton and some who were even worse. Help came from a surprising source when Sam Tyrell kicked Scranton in the groin. The six-gun exploded and bored a hole in the floor of the saloon, only inches from Scranton's right toecap.

Jack Almont was at a loss to

understand Tyrell's action. Had he been in his boss's boots, he'd have solved his dilemma by letting Scranton shoot Carty, and then by stringing Scranton up, thereby ingratiating himself with Lucy Carty by the swiftness of the justice delivered to her pa's killer.

But then he wasn't as besotted with Lucy Carty as Tyrell was. She was Tyrell's one weakness. More and more he was thinking about what impression his former hardman action would have on her, if he repeated his earlier methods of persuasion on the remaining ranchers who stood in the way of his ambitions.

While Tyrell was stepping back to a degree, Henry Scranton was becoming ever more rebellious. And after what Tyrell had just done he'd be storing up a lot more anger. Almont figured that if his plans for an easy street old age were not to be scuppered, he'd need to act soon. But try as he might, despite his frantic brainwork, no plan of action that would secure the future he wanted had come to mind. One would sooner or later present itself; that he knew. However, time was not on his side, so he was hoping that fate would serve up a plan of action pretty soon.

'You're prodding for trouble, Carty,' Tyrell growled. 'So you shouldn't be surprised if some day it comes calling at your door.'

'You want trouble, feel free to come calling any time, Tyrell,' Carty snarled. 'But I guess you ain't got that kinda mettle in ya, have ya? You'll send someone else to do your dirty work for you. Well,' he came toe to toe with Tyrell, 'whoever comes will surely leave feet first.'

'Let me sort this out for you right now, Mr Tyrell,' Almont said. 'You've got much more important things to do than deal with a pesky critter the likes of Carty.'

'He's a neighbour, Jack,' Tyrell said, feigning shock. 'And neighbours must learn to live with each other.'

'Not when one neighbour cuts off

water to the other, Tyrell,' Hank Carty spat.

'I've told you, Hank,' Tyrell said, as if trying to explain one more time to a dunderhead kid, 'you can have all the water you want.'

'At your price, Tyrell.'

'Ninety per cent of that water flows on my range, Hank. It's an asset. I'm a businessman, and businessmen make capital out of their assets. That's what businessmen do.'

'Water is God's gift, Tyrell. No one man's got a right to own it.'

'Well, if God saw fit to have that water cross my range before it reached yours, then he must have intended that I should benefit most from it. You reckon, Carty?'

'My stock is withering, Tyrell.'

'Getting real skinny,' Almont put in. 'Nothing but skin and bone soon.'

'Tell you what, Carty,' Tyrell offered, in the manner of a friend anxious to help. 'If you can't pay for the water in hard cash, then I'll do a deal on a land-for-water basis. Can't say fairer than that.' He turned to the crowd. 'Now can I, folks?'

'You made that offer before, Tyrell,' Carty barked. 'And second time round it's even more sour in my gut than it was first time. I ain't partin' with a single blade of grass to you!'

Sam Tyrell sneered. 'Then, my friend, you've got a real big problem, ain't you?'

'That's for sure,' Carty growled. 'And that problem's name is Sam Tyrell.'

'That sure sounds like a threat to me, Mr Tyrell,' Almont said. 'Seems to me that Carty intends to do you a mischief. Maybe I should cut off that mischief right now.'

'Don't talk nonsense, Almont,' Tyrell said. 'Old Hank here is all piss and wind. Ain't going to do nothing 'cept slip away quietly.' He stepped a couple of paces aside to give Almont a clear view of Carty. 'Ain't that so, neighbour?'

Hank Carty knew from the outset

that challenging Tyrell was going to be a risky business. To all appearances, Tyrell would seem, to one who didn't know about his rotten core, a man of compromising ways and accommodating nature. But a time or two Carty had seen him without his mask of bonhomie and good-fellowship, and had looked into a soul as black as hell's hobs. And only one thing would save him now from becoming wormbait, and that was for Sam Tyrell to maintain his false neighbourly persona until he owned every inch of the valley.

With Almont still in a drawing stance, the Broken Arrow saloon crackled with tension. A pin dropping to the floor would echo like a roll of mighty thunder. Hank Carty knew that he had handed his adversary an ace from the deck by his loose talk; talk that Almont had latched on to with the swiftness of his kind to carve out an opportunity to use the rig on his hips.

★ ★ ★

Don't say or do anything rash, Pa. Lucy Carty's words, spoken before he'd set out for town, echoed hollowly in Hank Carty's ears. He had assured her fervently that he would temper his speech and actions, but had then gone and done the exact opposite. *You can't stand up to Tyrell from the grave,* she'd cautioned, exhibiting the wisdom of her late mother, and delivering it with the same crinkle round the eyes and nose that Martha Carty, rest her good soul, would have shown. *Remember, Sam Tyrell is a snake-in-the-grass kind of man, Pa,* had been her parting warning.

'Don't fret so, gal,' he'd said impatiently. 'All I aim to do is to try and show Tyrell up for what he really is. A low-down land-grabber.'

'There'll be stew for supper,' Lucy had said. 'So be home on time. And no lingering in town supping with those cronies of yours.'

'Goddam, Lucy. It might be your ma standing right there!'

Lucy smiled, just like Martha Carty

used to. 'Thanks for the compliment, Pa.'

Hank returned her grin.

'And a compliment it surely is, Lucy,' he said sincerely. 'In fact the best compliment I could pay you, gal.' Riding away, he called back. 'And don't put too much salt in the darn stew.'

★ ★ ★

'If there's any chastising to be done,' Henry Scranton roared, straightening up. 'I'll do it!'

'Butt out, Henry!' Jack Almont snarled.

'Hell, no!' Scranton bellowed, his normally narrow eyes now mere evil slits.

'Both of you butt out.'

All eyes went to the batwings and Ben Allwood, the aged sheriff, who was hovering on close to retirement and was way out of his depth when it came to handling *hombres* like the hardcases Carty was standing up to.

14

Until Sam Tyrell's arrival in town a year previously, Lucky Hollow had been the kind of town where a kindly-natured man like Allwood could have drifted through the days sitting on a porch rocker, reminiscing about the more troubled times of his younger days as a lawman when Lucky Hollow had been a crossroads for different outlaw trails; a time before the town, under Ben Allwood's fists and guns, had become a burg that trail trash gave a wide berth to on their way to and from the border. But that was a long time ago, and the years separating the younger and older man had not been kind to Ben Allwood. Nowadays he rose from his chair a whole lot slower, and his gnarled hands did not reach his gun as quickly as in former times. When they did, his fingers had a way of missing the hammer, and if his thumb found the hammer his finger missed the trigger.

'And if I don't, Sheriff,' Almont sneered, knowing that there was little

Allwood could do to back up his demand.

'Then I guess I'll have to make you butt out, Almont,' Ben Allwood said sternly, but in his eyes there was a glint of apprehension that the gunslinger would push him.

Almont was dismissive.

'Go back to the law office and have a little snooze, Sheriff. I don't want to have to kill a half-crippled old man.'

Tyrell, quick to sense the latent sympathy for Allwood in the saloon's imbibers, knew that were he to yield to the temptation to allow Jack Almont to harm the sheriff, a lot of the ground-work he had put in in the town would vanish like smoke from a bottle, and that was the last thing he wanted. Individually, the citizens of Lucky Hollow did not amount to much, but collectively they could amalgamate into a force that would scupper his well-laid plans to own every blade of grass in the valley and every business in the town, and therefore everyone in town, too. So with these thoughts uppermost in his mind, Tyrell said:

'You fellas obey the law!'

It not being in their killer's nature, neither Jack Almont or Henry Scranton liked being stood down. But as jobs went, ramrodding in accordance with Tyrell's will in Lucky Hollow and the valley beyond, was about as easy money in the pocket as they would ever collect.

'You're the boss, boss,' Almont crooned.

'Yes, sir, Mr Tyrell. Like Jack says, you're the boss,' Scranton added.

'Sorry, Ben,' Tyrell apologized. 'The boys have had a drop too much. You understand.'

'Friends call me Ben, Tyrell,' Allwood said, his jaw granite. 'And you ain't no friend of mine.'

Sam Tyrell shrugged. 'If that's the way you want it, Sheriff,' he said easily.

'That's what I want, Tyrell,' the sheriff of Lucky Hollow confirmed. He switched his gaze to Hank Carty. 'It's getting late, you should be heading home, Hank. Lucy will worry that pretty head of hers to greyness.'

'Why don't you ride along with us, Carty?' Tyrell offered. 'There's safety in numbers.'

'I'd prefer to ride with the devil, Tyrell!' Hank Carty spat.

Tyrell swaggered past him on his way out of the saloon, his henchmen at his heels. 'Make sure you don't meet the devil on the way home, Carty.'

'If he does, I reckon the law will know where to find him, Tyrell,' Ben Allwood said.

Sam Tyrell snorted derisively and pushed past the lawman.

'Just a shot of whiskey and I'll be on my way, Ben,' Carty said.

'I've got a bottle in my desk drawer, Hank.'

Allwood turned and left.

2

A full bottle of Kentucky rye was standing dead centre of Allwood's desk when Hank Carty arrived at the sheriff's office. The lawman popped the cork and poured generously. He picked up his glass and saluted Carty. His swallow was long and pleasurable, and when he replaced his glass on the desk there was just a thimbleful of liquor remaining. Hank Carty's glass had about the same measure left when he set his glass down. Allwood poured again with the same generosity, but this time he sat and supped from his glass in a more measured manner. He chuckled. 'Near shit myself just now, Hank. How about you?'

'Same here,' Carty answered, joining Allwood in laughter. 'If you hadn't showed up, I reckon Tyrell would have let Almont off his leash. How did you know what was going on, Ben?'

'Art Clancy was visiting upstairs in the saloon. He saw what was about to happen from the top of the stairs as he made his way out through that door leading to the outside stairs that the less brazen clients of the Broken Arrow doves like to use. He legged it along here and told me.'

'I owe Art, big time,' Carty said.

Ben Allwood held up his glass and eyed Hank through its amber nectar. 'Pretty dumb, what you did, Hank. One day you'll ruffle Tyrell's feathers a mite too much, and that'll make him even meaner towards you than he already is, friend. You're prodding a rattler in Sam Tyrell.'

Allwood had been one of the few who had not been taken in by Tyrell. He was a shrewd, upright and honest badge-toter. His gunhand was long past its best, but his principles were still as untarnished as they had been when he'd taken his oath of office fifteen years previously. With this in mind, Carty said:

'You ain't in no fit position to lecture me, you old coot! If you stand in Tyrell's way, he'll not hesitate to put you six feet under either, Ben.'

The sheriff of Lucky Hollow did not argue with his friend's assessment. 'Thing is, Hank, I draw my pay to keep check on a fella like Tyrell.'

'Don't have no choice but to fight, Ben. You know Tyrell's plan to squeeze me out of the valley. And I damn well ain't going no place!'

'A man can leave in different ways, Hank. In a wagon, on a saddle, or in a pine box.' Allwood held up a hand to stay Carty's comeback. 'And you've got Lucy to think of. What d'ya suppose she'd do if you caught Tyrell's lead.'

'That land was nothing but dry dust when I came to the valley, Ben, you know that. Now it's fertile range, being turned back to dust again by Tyrell's antics in diverting the water.' Hank Carty's face set grimly. 'I worked hard to make my place what it is, and Martha, rest her soul, lies in that soil.'

He shook his head vehemently. 'And I ain't never going to leave her to rest alone, Ben. I'm planning on one day lying right 'longside her.'

Sheriff Ben Allwood's sigh was long and weary. 'Let's hope that it won't be sooner than you planned, Hank. Good whiskey.' He drained his glass. But the humour for socializing had completely deserted Carty, and he set his glass down on the desk.

'Guess I'd better make tracks, Ben.'

Allwood watched his old friend leave, his heart heavy that he could do nothing against the likes of Tyrell and his gunnies to help him. How he wished that he could wipe ten years off his age; that his hands didn't keep him awake nights with the intensity of the pain in their joints; that if he could manage it, he'd willingly stand with Hank Carty. In bucking Sam Tyrell his old friend would pay a terrible price, of that he was certain.

★　★　★

Riding out of town, Jack Almont complained, 'Why did you stay my hand, Mr Tyrell. I could have plucked a thorn from your side effortlessly just now.'

Sam Tyrell's mood was dour.

'You'll get your chance soon enough, Almont,' he promised. 'I'm growing real tired of Hank Carty's presence round here.'

'Just plug him and be done with, I say.'

'You might have a fast gunhand, Scranton,' Sam Tyrell growled. 'But you ain't the brightest wick to come down the line!'

From a slouching gait, Scranton came upright in his saddle, his back made ramrod-stiff by Tyrell's insult. 'Ain't no need for that kinda talk, Mr Tyrell,' he said, scowling.

'I pay your wages, Scranton,' Tyrell bellowed. 'So I'll damn well say what I like. You can settle for that or get to hell off my range and payroll!'

Noting the sneaky slide of Scranton's

hand to the left-sided gun of the double rig he wore, blind-side of Tyrell, and fearing being pitched out of easy pickings if Tyrell caught lead, Jack Almont quickly sought to quell the hostility that had built up between Tyrell and Scranton. 'Gents,' he crooned, 'seeing that we all want the same thing: Hank Carty out of the way, I don't see no point in us fellas gettin' all tetchy with each other.' Henry Scranton's spite-filled glare at Almont made clear his view of his partner's stab in the back intervention, as he saw it. He might have gone for his guns to seek reprisal for Almont's treachery, had the age-old question of who was faster been decided. But Scranton being a coward behind all the bluster and big talk, his nerve failed him. Nevertheless his spite and desire to square things with Jack Almont became all the more needful and urgent.

Had Almont not moved closer to Tyrell as a sign of where his loyalty would lie should lead start flying,

Henry Scranton's pride might have overruled his good sense. Instead, the words having to be forced out of his mouth, he said:

'Guess Jack's right, Mr Tyrell. Ain't no point in us fellas gettin' all tetchy with each other.' The hand he held out was rebuffed contemptuously by Sam Tyrell.

'You do exactly what I want, or pack up and ride out, Scranton!' Tyrell snarled, his narrow eyes filled with poison.

Expecting the worst outcome, Almont moved his horse between Scranton and Tyrell, looped the reins round his saddle horn, and let his hand hover over his gun in the clearest indication yet, if any were needed, of the side he was taking, but not out of any loyalty to Tyrell. He had got used to the lazy, well-paid existence Tyrell offered, of pushing gun-ignorant ranchers around in what amounted to a pussycat range war. Over the couple of months during which he had been Sam Tyrell's enforcer he had become used to drawing his pay with ease and being alive to spend it. He had been in other range wars where that was less certain and, now that he was getting that little bit longer in the tooth and slower on the draw, he'd choose Tyrell's version of range war any day. Of course there was the possibility that Hank Carty, stubborn cuss that he was proving to be, might change all of that by his determined resistance to Tyrell's plans. Or Scranton might be of a mind finally to put to the test which one of them was the faster, and he might find out that his opinion that *he* was, was the opinion of a fool.

While Jack Almont was thinking, Henry Scranton was having his thoughts also, and they were not unlike Almont's. With that in mind, he decided on diplomacy, to wait until he was on surer ground. 'Why don't we all just settle down, gents?' he said.

Relieved, Almont said, 'Seems a good idea to me, Mr Tyrell.'

Not wanting to lose a hardcase of Scranton's menace, Sam Tyrell, after an appropriate show of employer reluctance, agreed. 'Time for supper, I reckon,' he said. As he rode on into the gloom, his thoughts were of Hank Carty. Carty had the kind of spit in him that might attract others to his way of thinking, and that would make for all sorts of problems.

Carty was a problem he'd have to deal with soon. Real soon.

3

The man upon whom Sam Tyrell was pondering was at that moment poking the stew on his plate with his fork, decidedly uninterested in eating any of it, other than the first couple of mouthfuls he had taken fifteen minutes before, which now left the stew sitting on his plate an unappetizing sight. Looking up, he caught sight of his daughter's thunderous face and made a move to eat another mouthful of the gluttinous mess.

'Leave it,' Lucy Carty said, reaching over and grabbing the plate. 'The pig we're fattening will appreciate it, if you don't.'

'It's not that I don't appreciate your cooking, honey,' Carty pleaded. 'It's that all I've got on my mind's affecting my appetite.'

'Sure, Pa,' Lucy said, placatingly. 'I

understand. Coffee and pie?'

Carty shook his head. 'I think I'll have a whiskey, if you don't mind, Lucy.'

'No,' she replied, 'I don't mind.' But obviously she did. Her pa had begun a nightly ritual of going to bed liquored up shortly after he had buried her ma the year before, until now he seemed incapable of ignoring the bottle of rotgut that was as essential a purchase when he went to town as household necessities. It saddened her deeply to see him slip away into what would become, if he did not quit soon, a permanent state of whiskey stupor. She had tried to talk to him about his drinking, but every time she tried to raise the subject he shrewdly anticipated her attempt and side-stepped it. She knew that soon there would be no other course open to her than to pin him down and have it out. If he was not of a mind to listen she would probably have to up and leave, if she could muster that amount of courage. 'You're all Hank's got now, honey,' had been her ma's dying words. 'Be kind to him. I need to know that you'll keep him safe for me until the time comes for me to come back and gather him to me again.' Since they had been spoken her ma's words had burned more and more into her brain, rendering her powerless to act.

'I'm beat, honey,' Carty said. 'Think I'll take to my bed, if'n that's OK with you?'

'Sure, Pa. You sleep well.'

When he had left the kitchen Lucy wept until she had no more tears left to cry. 'Oh, Ma,' she wailed, 'what am I to do?'

★ ★ ★

Lucy Carty watched the full moon drift across the sky through her bedroom window. She was still full of worry about how she could save her pa from his folly and the ranch from falling into Sam Tyrell's hands.

'There's one sure way,' Tyrell had told her when their paths had crossed the last time she'd been to town. 'Marry me, Lucy. That way your pa keeps what he's got, and I'll cut off another hundred acres or so to add to his. Pretty generous, don't you think?'

It would have been if she could even like Tyrell. The fact was, he made her skin crawl. But, she thought despondently, in time marrying Sam Tyrell might be the only option open to her. Behind the sugar-coated blather she knew that Tyrell would sooner or later tire of waiting to fulfil his ambitions, show his true colours, and use his hardcase outfit to ramrod his will on the valley.

Her response on this occasion had had more thorns than a rose bush. 'I'd rather hitch myself to a rattler, Sam Tyrell.' She'd shaken off his restraining hand on her arm. 'Some things carry too high a price to be even considered,' she'd said, setting her buggy in motion with a flick of the whip she would have preferred to lay across Tyrell's cheek.

He'd laughed. 'Someday you might have no choice other than to accept my terms, Lucy.' The truth of his statement stung her deeply. Then he added tersely, 'If I'm still of a mind to make an offer.'

She had left Lucky Hollow that day, heavy-hearted and determined never to give the least consideration to Sam Tyrell's offer. But, slowly, as she made her way home she began to see a whole lot of sense in his proposition, dark and depressing as that sense was. Tying the knot with Sam Tyrell would solve a whole mess of problems, and probably prevent her pa from catching lead because of his mule-headed bucking of Tyrell. She had little doubt that, if her pa continued to drum up resistance to Sam Tyrell, there would come a point when Tyrell would move to quieten him. And there was the ever present danger that one of that blackhearted pair, Jack Almont and Henry Scranton, would take her pa's demise into their own hands.

'Oh, moon,' she sighed. 'Wouldn't I just love to be up there, away from all this trouble.' Then, drifting into sleep, she murmured, 'I'm sure trying as hard as I can, Ma, to do as you wanted me to do. But it ain't easy.'

★　★　★

Lucy came awake with a start, not knowing what had woken her. A wind had come up, sighing round the house like a dying breath, squeezing into nooks and crannies and crevices, giving the impression of wandering ghosts.

She got out of bed and went to the window to look out on the back yard, which her bedroom overlooked. That the moon had taken to dancing behind the gathering storm clouds, mischievously filling the yard with shadows that had a life of their own, annoyed her. She let her gaze drift across the yard, examining every shadow for sinsister meaning until she was satisfied that there was none, before she returned to bed. She listened for a while longer, and was on the verge of drifting into sleep again when she heard the creak of what she suspected was the henhouse door, directly across the yard from her window. That was not unusual in itself, but this time it sounded as if it was eased open or shut in a manner that the blustery wind would not have managed.

She hurried along the hall to her pa's room without much hope of waking him; his snoring was deep and even, which indicated a deep drunken sleep; there would be no stirring Hank Carty. There was nothing for it but to check out the yard and henhouse herself, not a very inviting prospect. She went downstairs to the kitchen where she took a rifle from the rack near the door and went outside into the windswept night.

* * *

Across the valley Sam Tyrell was pacing back and forth across his parlour, gripped by another spell of anxiety that his plans for control of the valley and beyond were not going as smoothly as he had reckoned they should when he had added Henry Scranton and Jack Almont to his payroll. A couple of farmers and small ranchers had opted to pull out, fearing the trouble that lay ahead with men like Scranton and Almont; however most, taking courage from Hank Carty's defiant stand, had stayed put, at least until they saw how Tyrell came out against their feisty hard-talking neighbour. It troubled him that his paid agents among the valley dwellers who were privy to the meetings which Carty had arranged with his fellow strugglers against him had reported a steady growth in support for Carty's stand. The most recent report from his agent conveyed the disturbing news that there was a hardening attitude of resistance to him, orchestrated by Carty. The agent had opined that allowing Carty to continue to spout off would create a resistance that would be costly to break and might not be broken at all. If that happened he'd have to leave the valley with his tail between his legs, and he'd be damned if he'd be run out.

He went to the front door and hollered out to the bunkhouse for Jack Almont to come to the house. He had decided that someone needed to be taught a lesson. If a couple of barns went up in smoke it might encourage the ranchers and farmers who were cosying up to Hank Carty's revolutionary gab to pull back and sell up. For a brief moment he had thought about teaching Carty a lesson directly, but reckoned that any ensuing sympathy for him would only, in the long run, gather more support for his stand.

'You hollered, boss?' Henry Scranton said, stepping into the parlour.

'Not for you, Scranton,' Tyrell said gruffily.

'Almont ain't 'round.'

'Not around?' Tyrell barked. 'Where is he?'

36

'Don't know.'

'What d'ya mean, you don't know? You bunk side by side with Almont.'

'He was right there when I dozed off an hour ago. Then when you hollered and I woke, he wasn't there no more. He was real restless earlier.'

'Restless? What d'ya mean by restless, Scranton?'

Scranton shrugged. 'Jack's got his . . . longings, boss. And sometimes those longings get so bad that they can't be handled. I know he's been eyein' up that new filly in the saloon in town.'

Sam Tyrell came and stood toe to toe with his hireling. 'Anyone else Almont's been eyeing up, Scranton?' he barked.

Again, Henry Scranton shrugged. 'There's been the Widow Hollins — '

'And?'

'Lucy Carty, boss.' Henry Scranton grabbed his chance to put in the poison. 'Jack was sayin' just the other day that he had plans for her; plans that he said he'd carry through whether she liked them or not. When he's in a mood, not many women like Jack's plans, Mr Tyrell.'

'Find him!' Tyrell ordered. 'And if he's harmed Lucy Carty, hang him.'

'Hang him? Why waste a good rope. I could . . . ' Henry Scranton's hands caressed his guns.

Tyrell snorted. 'Hanging's more certain, Scranton.'

'That remains to be seen, Mr Tyrell,' the gunslinger said stiffly, his face suffused with offence.

'You've got your orders!' Tyrell snapped.

'Sure, boss,' Scranton said.

'Then go and do as I say, Scranton.'

Henry Scranton backed off. For a terrifying moment Sam Tyrell thought that he was going to do for him. His relief was immense when the gunslinger turned and stormed out, his back ramrod stiff with injured pride and humble pie.

★ ★ ★

Lucy Carty's journey across the yard was a cautious one, cleverly using the darkness to progress when the moon went behind a cloud. The lonely night wind swept across the yard, clutching at her as if intent on pulling her out into the open. A wormbait nag to the side of the henhouse shifted uneasily. On reaching the henhouse, she steadied herself, and levelled the rifle.

4

'Come out, whoever you are!' she ordered. There was no response. 'That door ain't bullet proof,' she said. 'Neither are the walls. If I start shooting, chances are you'll catch lead.' Still no response. 'You ain't leaving me much choice,' she called out, above a sudden gust of wind that almost unbalanced her. 'I don't want to lay you low, but I will, if by the count of three I don't see your face. One . . . two . . thr . . . ' The door creaked open and a man, made lanky by hunger, Lucy reckoned, stepped forward. 'Fingers to the sky, mister!'

The man did as Lucy ordered.

'What's your name?'

'Tod Lacey.'

'What're you doing, skulking?'

'It's a henhouse. I was hoping to find some eggs.'

'Hungry?'

'Damn hungry,' he said. His voice was surprisingly deep, emanating from a near-skeletal frame.

'Where do you hail from?'

'Here and there, and no place, ma'am.'

'What're you doing in these parts?'

He grinned. 'You sure do ask a lot of questions, don't you.'

'You're on Carty property. I'm holding the gun. That gives me the right, mister.'

'Guess it does at that.'

'So what're you doing round these parts?'

'Passing through.'

Somehow she could believe him. He wore no gun. Stood in what amounted to rags. His boots were long past their best, and his horse wasn't in any better shape than he was. There was no way that this scarecrow specimen could be in Sam Tyrell's employ.

'Find any eggs?'

'No ma'am.'

'Hens ain't been laying good these past weeks.'

'Pity. If you lower that rifle I'll be on my way, ma'am. Is there a town hereabouts?'

'That'll be Lucky Hollow. About six miles east of here.'

'Obliged.'

There was no way, it seemed, that he would make it as far as town, and her heart went out to him as he vanished into the night.

'Hey,' she called out impulsively, hoping that she was doing the right thing. He was a stranger and therefore he could be a danger, was the unwritten law of the West.

The man who called himself Tod Lacey appeared back out of the dark. 'Ma'am?'

'I've got some eggs in the house if you want them.'

'That's very generous,' he said. 'And I'd be mighty grateful.'

'Then come on inside. But . . . '

'But, ma'am?'

'I'll be holding this rifle on you every second of your visit. Is that agreeable.'

'I don't have a choice,' Lacey said. 'So I guess I'm agreeable.'

'You go on ahead. Blink an eye and you won't go no further, Mr Lacey,' she warned. Going inside to the kitchen, she said, 'There's a lamp on the dresser to your left. Light it.'

'Yes, ma'am.'

The glow of lamplight showed the stranger to be even more down at heel than he had appeared in the shadows in the yard. His face was gaunt with hunger. The rags he wore were clothes that were tailored originally to fit a man of much broader stature. His dark hair was uncut and looped in a fringe almost down to his right cheekbone. However, down-at-heel as he looked, his person was, discounting trail dust, spotlessly clean.

Lucy Carty saw a man who had fallen from a great height to his present pitiful state. However she remained at the ready for trouble and kept him steadfastly under threat of the cocked 'Chester. She had come across evil wretches before who were ace actors. 'Got to help yourself,' she said. 'Bacon and eggs are to hand.'

The man's hand went involuntarily to rub his sunken stomach. His gaunt parody of a grin hinted at a one-time handsome man with an easy and ready smile. 'Have I died and gone to heaven?'

'Hell, maybe!' Hank Carty, bleary-eyed, one hand holding a cocked six-gun shaking dangerously, stepped into the kitchen. His whiskey-reddened eyes glared at his daughter. 'Why didn't you use that 'Chester the minute you set eyes on this *hombre*, Lucy?'

'Gave me no cause to, Pa,' she returned hotly, embarrassed by Carty's interrogation in the presence of Lacey. 'If you hadn't been out cold when I called you, maybe you would have.'

'Don't sass me, gal!' Carty bellowed.

'I'm a grown woman, Pa. And I know what I'm doing,' she flung back, giving no ground.

Hank Carty growled, 'Well, best shoot him now to be safe.'

Carty took unsteady aim.

'He's unarmed, Pa,' Lucy said urgently. She could not believe that her pa would shoot Tod Lacey down in cold blood, but at that moment, seeing a crazy light in his eyes that she had never seen before, she could not be certain. She stepped between Lacey and her pa. 'You'll have to shoot through me, if it's killing Mr Lacey you want, Pa.'

What Hank Carty saw as his daughter's mistake was, it seemed, just that, when Lacey's left arm looped round her waist to use her as a shield, while his right hand grabbed the rifle she held.

Stunned by what was a wholly unexpected turn of events, Lucy Carty looked back at Lacey, an ocean of disappointment in her blue eyes.

'Drop the gun, mister!' he rasped. 'Or I'll drop you for sure.' Carty did as ordered.

'Sorry, Pa.' Lucy wept.

'Nothing to be sorry for, Lucy. Like your ma before you, you have a good and kind heart that scum take advantage of.' His eyes bore into Tod Lacey with the intensity of hot coals. 'You're a poor specimen, if ever I saw one,' he said. 'Sam Tyrell's scraping the bottom of the barrel when he's hiring scarecrows to do his bidding.'

'Tyrell? Don't know any Sam Tyrell,' Lacey said.

'A liar as well as a killer,' Carty snorted.

'I ain't no liar, mister,' Lacey grated. 'Neither am I a killer.' Much to Hank Carty's surprise, he set Lucy Carty free and handed back her Winchester. He repeated: 'Like I said. I ain't no liar. And I ain't no killer.'

Lucy Carty slapped him hard across the face, and stated, 'No man puts his hands on me uninvited!'

Tod Lacey rubbed his smarting left cheek. 'I guess I ain't likely to forget that, ma'am,' he said wryly. He rubbed his cheek again. 'Not for quite a spell at the very least.'

46

Lucy Carty's fury suddenly dissipated and she laughed heartily, thinking that Tod Lacey's arm had felt mighty comfortable round her waist. But it was a thought that she quickly dismissed. This man was a shiftless drifter.

There was something in his daughter's laughter and in her gait, too, as she faced the stranger that worried Hank Carty.

'Those eggs and bacon are still on offer, Mr Lacey,' she said, without consulting Carty. Conscious of her disregard for his right to respect, Lucy said by way of apology, 'If that's OK with you, Pa?'

'It's OK,' he said. 'But I expect you to be on your way when you've done eating, mister. Agreed?'

Following Carty's line of vision to his daughter, and understanding perfectly the basis for his concern, Tod Lacey said, 'I wasn't figuring on staying round, sir.'

'It's the middle of the night, Tod,' Lucy said, concerned. His daughter's soft use of the stranger's first name was not lost on Hank Carty. 'At least wait until first light. You can bunk down in the barn.'

'I'll say who can bunk down in the barn!' Carty barked. 'This man — '

'Tod's his name,' Lucy interjected spiritedly, goaded by her pa's rebuke. 'Tod Lacey.'

'Well, I'm sure Mr Lacey will have a keen hankering to be on his way as soon as he's grubbed,' Carty said, in a tone of voice that did not invite a retort.

'I prefer to sleep under the stars, ma'am,' Lacey said. 'Don't take much to having a roof over me. I like to look up and imagine someone looking back at me.'

Just then there was a rush of rain against the kitchen window.

'Ain't no stars. There's a downpour just beginning,' Lucy said. 'Been in the wind these last couple of days. Trails will vanish under a downpour.'

'I ain't no amateur in finding my way,' Lacey said. 'I'd welcome a full belly, and then a quick departure, ma'am.'

'A quick departure,' Lucy said stiffly. 'You would, would you? Then that's what you'll have. I'll get those bacon and eggs ready right now.'

'Obliged ma'am.'

Lucy thought she heard a note of regret in Tod Lacey's voice. But how could that be, with him so eager to leave her company? Never were eggs and bacon so angrily cooked and presented. 'Guess now that my womanly chores have been completed, I can go back to bed,' Lucy said, making to leave the kitchen.

'Bye, ma'am,' Lacey said. 'Sure grateful to you.'

'Doing my Christian duty, Mr Lacey, that's all. Feeding the hungry.' The kitchen door slammed behind her, fit to split from its frame.

'A spirited girl you've got there, sir,' Lacey told Hank Carty.

'Got the same spit as her ma had,' Carty said, hanging his head to hide the tears that threatened to spill from his eyes.

'Saw the cross on that patch to the side of the house,' Lacey said.

''Sunny side', that's what she said, when she was leaving. 'Plant me on the sunny side of the house, Hank. That way I won't be cold while I'm waiting for you to join me'.'

'You miss her a lot, huh?'

'Sure do,' he said. 'Always will as long as I'm sucking air. Which,' his eyes became reflective, 'might not be much longer the way things are going round here.'

'Trouble?'

'Yeah. Lots of trouble.'

'From the owner of that big house I passed on the other side of the valley on my way here?' Tod Lacey shrewdly guessed.

'That would be the Tyrell house. Sam Tyrell's got a mountain of ambition, seems set to collect every pebble to make up that mountain, and he don't much mind how.'

'And you're standing in his way?'

'As he sees it,' Carty said.

'And how do you see it?' Lacey asked.

'I see it as having a right to hold on to what's mine, and not letting go of it 'cause another man reckons he should have it to add to his lot.'

'And Mr Tyrell disagrees?'

'Surely does.'

'It's a brave stand you've taken.'

Hank Carty laughed mirthlessly. 'Brave, huh? Foolhardy is the opinion of most round here.'

'Most could have a point,' Lacey stated. 'Hot lead usually follows on hot argument in this kind of ruckus.'

'Know a lot about this kind of ruckus, Lacey?' Carty enquired suspiciously.

'Some,' Lacey replied neutrally.

'How much would some be?' Carty persisted.

'I've been involved in a couple of range wars.'

'Is that a fact?' Carty said coldly.

'Not a pretty sight, range running red with blood.'

Hank Carty's interest in Lacey, which had been waning, came back with a bang. 'Did you do a lot of spilling of this blood?'

Lacey considered the question before answering. 'A fairish share.'

Carty shifted in his chair.

'Maybe you didn't just see that big house, mister,' he grated. 'Maybe you was in it. And maybe,' he levelled the six-gun he was still holding on Tod Lacey, 'you talked to Tyrell some 'bout a range war in this neck of the woods.'

'No, I didn't,' Lacey answered unequivocally.

'Now how can I be sure of that?'

'You can't,' Tod Lacey stated bluntly. 'You take my word for it, or you don't, simple as that.' He stood up from the table.

'Easy,' Carty warned.

'I mean you no harm, sir,' Lacey said. 'But if you reckon I do, then use that shooter. And if you reckon I don't, set it

52

aside. Your choice.'

Tension eddied dangerously back and forth between the men, before Hank Carty placed the pistol on the table. 'Best get the last of that grub inside you before it goes cold. Then I'll see you to the barn. It ain't no hotel, but it'll be better than the trail on a night like this.' His eyes held Lacey's. 'But if you want to head out, I won't twist your arm to stay, neither.'

'First light be OK?'

'Dandy.'

'Then you've got yourself a grateful overnight guest, sir.'

'Don't let that gratefulness extend to creeping back into the house, Lacey,' Carty growled.

'No, sir.'

'That's our deal, then?'

'That's our deal,' Tod Lacey agreed.

★ ★ ★

As the kitchen door opened Jack Almont, his face as twisted as Satan's on a bad day (deprived as he had been of his planned visit to Lucy Carty, even if it meant stepping over her pa's dead body to achieve it) sank back into the shadows at the side of the house. As Carty escorted Lacey to the barn, Almont wondered who the stranger might be; he also wondered why a man whose hips were made for a gunbelt, and whose gait suggested that up to recent times that was what had adorned them, was doing hobnobbing with Hank Carty.

Could it be that Carty had got hold of a gunnie?

As Almont watched Hank Carty and the stranger, he himself was being watched by Henry Scranton. When Carty entered the barn with the stranger Almont took his chance to sneak away to his waiting horse. In a sudden glimmer of moonlight his scowl was plain to see. He walked his horse a distance from the house before mounting up. With Almont gone and Carty and the stranger in the barn, Scranton hurried to the house and entered with the stealth of a ghost. He crept along the narrow hall and made his way upstairs. It was not difficult to find Carty's bedroom, he just had to follow the smell of stale rotgut. He entered the room, he went straight to the pocket of Carty's vest and found in the pocket what he needed to lend authenticity to the evil plan he had hatched while watching Almont. As he went back downstairs, Henry Scranton's grin was ear-to-ear wide. Certain now that his plan would work, he lost no time in hogging his cohort's tail. Rake-thin as compared to Almont's beefiness, his passage over the rocky trail skirting the valley was ghostly. A short distance into the trail, he took an off-shoot over which he could ride faster to come out on the trail ahead of Almont. Riding into the moonlight, the clouds having drifted away, Scranton had a sly grin. It seemed that events had conveniently favoured him. In the hawkish land that was the West, the man who was favoured by Lady Luck was usually the man who survived. So, as Henry Scranton reached the curve on the trail where he planned to waylay Jack Almont and secure his own future, he was confident that good fortune was his.

* * *

'Ain't much,' Hank Carty said, on observing Tod Lacey's eye being cast over the barn, if barn in the real meaning of the word could be applied to the confined space that obviously served as a general disposal area. 'I've been planning a new barn, but the time ain't been right for a spell. A fella by the name of Sam Tyrell reckons that me and my neighbours should up roots and leave every blade of grass round here for his expanding herd,' he explained in response to Lacey's quizically raised left eyebrow.

'Range trouble ain't easy to deal with,' Lacey said. 'Can mean a whole mess of blood being spilled, over some-thing that has to be settled in the long run anyway.' He held Hank Carty's gaze, which had become frostier.

'So I guess you'd up and let a bastard like Tyrell have free rein to do whatever it pleased him to do, huh?' Carty made no attempt to hide his contempt for Lacey, figuring him to be a tail-turner, a species he had always held to be beneath contempt.

'I didn't say that,' Lacey said, with a degree of rancour.

'Then what are you saying, mister?' Carty challenged.

'I guess I'm saying that being buried in the soil of this valley ain't going to do you or your daughter any good. And that's the price you might have to pay for bucking this fella Tyrell.'

Worry masked Hank Carty's face.

'I ain't worried about me,' he said, troubled. 'But I surely fret about Lucy.'

'You should worry about yourself too,' Tod Lacey said, 'Because from what I've seen in our brief acquaintance is a crusty, mule-stubborn man who's putting a ton of worry on her young shoulders, which might be every bit as fatal as hot lead.'

Hank Carty knew the truth of Lacey's reading of the story, but his reaction was far from revealing that.

'Mister,' he growled, 'you ain't nothing more than a trail bum looking for a handful of clean straw to rest on. So don't tell me the way I should do things round here!' He glared at Lacey. 'You'll be on your way come first light.'

'Never planned on staying around,' Lacey said. 'In fact,' he crossed to the door, 'I'll be on my way right now, I reckon.'

He was halfway across the yard when Carty hailed him. 'I've got enough problems without Lucy taking my skin off come breakfast time,' he said. He shoved in the door of the barn by way of invitation to Lacey to reconsider his departure.

'Wouldn't want to upset the lady,' Lacey said.

Hank Carty chuckled. 'You and me both, Lacey.' He crossed himself. 'When bucked, that gal's got a temper that would put legs under Satan hisself.'

Re-entering the barn, his grin wide, Tod Lacey remarked: 'How come such an old goat like you produced a sweet-as-honey daughter?'

''Cause she had a ma, rest her soul, sweet as honey before her. All she got from me is her temper. You ain't got a gun,' he observed. 'Come to the house and fetch one.'

'Don't like guns.'

'Huh?' Carty questioned, utterly bewildered.

'They kill people, and they don't care who it is. Just anyone who gets in the way.'

'In this valley lead is as common as muck,' Carty said. 'So are men who don't have any qualms about slinging it at anyone who gets in the way. And that includes fellas who have no stake in the valley. But, being a guest of a fella who does, they might prefer to make sure, Lacey.'

'Appreciate your concern.'

'I ain't concerned,' Carty flung back as he walked away, beckoning Lacey to follow him back to the house.

Chuckling, Lacey followed. Carty, on entering the kitchen, enquired, 'Shotgun, pistol or rifle?' And added immediately, 'Darn fool question. There's only one weapon for a fella who ain't gun-handy.' He selected a shotgun from the gunrack. 'The point-and-pull kind.' He handed Lacey the blunderbus. 'If any bastard shows up try to hit him square in the belly. Soft tissue slows buckshot. Real painful, that.'

'Sleep well,' he called after Lacey when he left. 'Oh, and if I catch you inside the house, I'll kill you,' he added matter-of-factly.

'Don't doubt it,' Lacey flung back, and closed the door of the barn.

Hank Carty did not close the kitchen door for a spell, but stood looking towards the barn in deep thought. 'Something about him that ain't right,' he murmured, and reckoned he had been the fool of all fools to hand the stranger a shotgun, because in so doing he could forget about sleep. Tod Lacey moved in a fashion that belied his trail-trash persona. Casting his mind back to when he had handed him the shotgun, he recalled that Lacey had handled the blaster with a whole pile of know-how and respect — the kind of respect a man who knew the devastating power of such a lethal weapon would possess. His next thought was profoundly troubling.

Might Sam Tyrell have cleverly placed an enemy in camp?

5

Henry Scranton was becoming impatient, reckoning that Jack Almont should have long since reached where he was lying in wait for him. There was an old trail over the hills that was a roundabout way of reaching the Circle T but, like him, Almont was a relative newcomer to the territory, so it would be unlikely that he'd chose an unfamiliar trail, lit only by a fickle moon. Besides, he had heard that the hill trail, an old defunct outlaw passage to the border, was in a poor state of repair. However, it was well known that it was Almont's impulsive and unpredictable nature, his knack for springing surprise, that had saved his hide more than once. Maybe his quirkiness had once again saved him from the treachery Scranton was planning. There was also the chance that he had veered off and headed for Lucky Hollow. But it was late to make the journey, and most of the saloon girls would by now have been bedded or be in the process of doing a deal with that end in mind.

About to quit, Scranton heard the rattle of shale close by. He ducked behind a boulder beside the trail. Almont rounded a bend. A shaft of moonlight crossing his face showed a grim visage; the expression of a man whose ambitions had been thwarted. Normally a cautious and canny customer, always aware of his surroundings and any danger that might be present, Almont's disguntlement and his thoughts of what his pleasure might have been had he successfully entered the Carty house, made him less wary than usual, which Scranton was mighty thankful for. Though he'd have the edge over his fellow gunnie, even preoccupied as Almont was, his survival instincts would quickly kick in. That was why Henry Scranton was a relieved and happy man that he had taken the time to become as proficient with a knife as a gun. The lessons he had taken from a Mexican *bandido* with whom he had formed a brief alliance would now pay off. The alliance with the Mex had been brief because, after a stage robbery that yielded an unexpectedly rich haul, Scranton had decided to use his new skill when the *bandido* turned his back on him.

He crouched as low as he could; it would have been better if he could lie flat on his belly, but rising from such a position would be less swift than springing from a crouch and infinitely more dangerous because it could not be achieved with the same degree of stealth. Nor would it give him the spring he would need to sling a knife with enough force when Almont passed by to overcome the distance and sink the blade into Almont's back with sufficient deadliness to at least disable him for long enough for Scranton to slit Almont's throat, if needs be.

Unsuspecting, Jack Almont rode on: a fly into a spider's web. But just when it seemed that his murderous plan could be successfuly implemented, the fickle moonlight switched direction, sending a creeping shaft of light snaking along towards Scanton.

★　★　★

On his way back to bed Hank Carty looked in on his daughter, who was tossing restlessly in her sleep; a restlessness that worried Carty no end. Lucy was at a foolish age between girl and woman: an age when a man like Tod Lacey could make a big impression. As he stood now, having the scrawniness of poor grubbing and caked with trail-dust, Lacey was no oil-painting, but Carty, from long experience of sizing men up, could see another man behind the outward one, and what he saw was a man who not too long ago had been a fine cut of a fella, the kind of *hombre* who would start a chain reaction in the ladies. Lucy would not have seen the man Tod

Lacey had once been, but inside, deep down in her femininity an earthquake just might be starting up.

It was at times like this that he wished that Martha, his beloved wife, was around to talk woman talk with Lucy; talk that he couldn't even begin to get his mouth around; talk that Lucy would shush if he even tried. But there would be no need of such talk. Come first light Lacey would ride on. Carty would even cut out a horse from the corral to replace the poor specimen of horseflesh Lacey was riding to help him on his way, and that would be that. Lucy would have a couple of bad days, and then she'd settle down again.

At least, that was his hope. But he'd seen how women reacted to men like Lacey. There was something in women that had them flitting about no-goods like moths round a flame, bereft of their good sense. He had his regrets about having let Lacey stay overnight. But he figured that if he had not, then Lucy would, like her ma before her, become stubborn, and in his experience there was nothing as difficult to handle as a woman with a set mind. The Carty women had strong minds and even stronger wills that took poorly to any man dictating terms to them.

With any luck, Tod Lacey would be long gone before Lucy woke up.

He closed her door quietly and went on his way to his own bed. Stretched out, watching the moon drift past outside his window, Hank Carty said, 'If you can hear me, Martha honey, I want you to help me with this, if'n I need help, and I reckon I will, aplenty too.' He drifted into sleep, resisting reaching for the bottle of whiskey that nowadays had become a permanent aid to finding sleep.

* * *

'Come on!' Henry Scranton murmured anxiously when Almont slowed his pace, and the shaft of moonlight crept closer and closer to where he lay in wait to do his deed of murder.

Almont turned in his saddle to check the trail behind him and, finding it empty, turned to look to either side suspiciously. Scranton's breath caught in his craw. Almont had no good reason to check on his surroundings, so the only reason for Almont's sudden edginess was his instinctive feel for trouble; instinct that had been honed razor sharp over many years, many trails, and a whole passel of trouble. They would be instincts which Almont had come to trust.

Almont drew rein. Listened. Watched.

Scranton crouched lower still but, alerted, Almont would have the eyes of a cat and the senses of a predator. Meanwhile, inch by inch the shaft of moonlight crept relentlessly on, and Scranton began to fear for the first time that the tables might be turning, that it would be Jack Almont who would ride away.

6

Sam Tyrell paced back and forth, checking first his pocket timepiece, then rechecking the clock on the wall of his den. It had been almost two hours since he had ordered Henry Scranton to find Jack Almont. It took at most an hour to make the round trip to the Carty place and town, and it worried him that Almont or, worse, Almont and Scranton together had decided to take their pleasure with Lucy Carty. The fate of any other woman in town or valley would not have raised a concern in him, but he had ambitions to one day take Lucy as his wife, and that would not be possible if she had been soiled by two no-goods like Almont and Scranton.

He tried to console himself with the possibility that Scranton had found Almont in town and that they had decided to dally with a couple of saloon doves, but he doubted that. Scranton would have, because he was ill-disciplined and impetuous, but Jack Almont was a cagey sort and seldom if ever in the time he had been in his pay, had he seen him act without thinking. Almont was a man who measured his responses, and only acted when the risk to his well-being was at its least. For the time being both Almont and Scranton had their uses.

However when the dust settled and it came to a parting of the ways, Scranton would be his choice as a ramrod; he would have no hesitation in snuffing out any trouble should it arise, which it probably would, because powerful men always attracted trouble of one kind or another. And Tyrell reckoned that Scranton was also the man to deal with Almont when that gent needed per-suading to forsake his ambitions; ambitions which he thought were secret, but which Sam Tyrell, well versed in skullduggery, was instinctively aware of. Henry Scranton might not be as fast as Jack Almont, but he was a hell of a lot craftier.

But all of that was in the future. Right now, if there was trouble between Scranton and Almont, or if they had gotten round to thinking that as a pair in partnership they'd be better than as odd singles, their combined ambition might become a bigger problem than every farmer and rancher in the valley put together. Up to now he had cleverly kept Scranton and Almont at odds with each other by favouring one and then the other, and holding out the hope to both that one day they would figure prominently as part of the Circle T.

As individuals they were dangerous men. As a twosome they would be a deadly duo.

★　★　★

Tod Lacey lay awake, and he knew the reason why: Lucy Carty. He had drifted with no sense of purpose, loaded down with the guilt of the past, unable to come to terms with one awful event that had changed his entire life. He neither sought or wanted company and stuck in the main (except when it was absolutely necessary) to out of the way places and trails that were more or less his alone to traverse. He didn't seek company, and didn't want it either. The sole purpose of his visit to the Carty ranch had been to steal a batch of eggs from the henhouse to fill a hollow belly.

And then he had seen Lucy Carty.

★ ★ ★

'Anyone there?' Jack Almont called out.

Scranton dared not breathe.

'I figure there is. Show yourself now and that'll be an end of it. But keep skulking and I'll flush you out and kill you.' Almont's gaze scanned all round him. 'Last chance. I'm fast with a gun and equally so with my brain. So I figure the odds are stacked against you, friend.'

Suddenly fearful, for a couple of

seconds Henry Scranton toyed with the idea of stepping out and making a joke of hiding. But would Almont buy it? He doubted that he would. So there was nothing to do but hold out and hope that Almont would come forward the hundred yards that would take him past his hiding place. He could not shoot Almont, because no one would believe that Hank Carty would get the drop on the gunfighter with a pistol.

Almont slid from his saddle.

'I'm comin' to flush you out, friend. So if you've got any words that you hope will get you through the pearly gates, now is the time to utter them.'

Henry Scranton had a dilemma. The shaft of moonlight was almost upon him and he would be revealed. Now that Almont had dismounted he was not as large a target. All in all, that left him with only one option and that was to play an idiot's card.

He showed himself.

★　★　★

Like Tod Lacey, Lucy Carty tossed and turned also, every inch of her once comfortable mattress and pillow seemingly full of stones. She came up with at least a hundred good reasons for her restlessness, before she sat up in bed and admitted to herself that Tod Lacey was the one and only reason for her agitation. Scrawny as he was, he was not much to look at, and even padded out he would still not turn too many heads, but somehow he had got inside her and was twisting her guts into knots and spinning her mind like a straw in the wind.

In the room next to hers Hank Carty listened to her toss and turn, and knew that his worry about the effect Lacey had had on his daughter was well-founded. That made it imperative that when she rose from her restless slumber, Lacey would be long gone.

He got up and dressed.

* * *

Sam Tyrell stopped his frantic pacing, went and opened the front door and crossed to the bunkhouse. 'Larry. Saul.' Two men stretched out on their bunks stood up. 'Saddle up.'

'Trouble, boss?' Saul asked.

'Remains to be seen,' Tyrell answered glumly. He turned to leave. 'Meet me out front of the house in no more than five minutes.'

'Sure, Mr Tyrell,' Larry said.

★ ★ ★

'Howdy Jack.' Henry Scranton greeted Almont skittishly. 'Got you goin' there, friend.'

Jack Almont at first remained impassive. Then a slow smile spread across his mouth. 'Horsin' round ain't your style, Henry. How come you suddenly took to it, huh?'

Scranton's hand holding the knife behind his back was clammy with sweat. If he did not use the knife soon it would become useless.

'What're you doin' out here at dead of night?' Almont asked.

'Felt like taking some fresh air, instead of hangin' round that stinkin' bunk-house.'

'Fresh air, huh?'

'Yeah,' Scranton replied unconvincingly.

'The Carty place is just a mile on 'long the trail. You hadn't it in mind to pay a visit to Lucy Carty, now had you, Henry?'

Scranton laughed. 'You know, Jack, I gotta be honest. Lucy Carty did come to mind.'

'Horseshit!' Almont cursed. 'I'm guessin' that when Tyrell went lookin' and I wasn't there to find, he put two and two together and figured that I was sniffin' round Lucy Carty. Ain't that so, Henry?'

'I ain't privy to Tyrell's thoughts, Jack.'

'And, him being real keen to be the first to crack Lucy open, he sent you to spoke my wheel. Ain't that so,' Almont queried angrily.

The spittal in Scranton's mouth dried up.

'Ain't so, Jack. Like I said — '

'You're out for fresh air, right?' Almont mocked.

'That's right.'

'Liar!'

Scranton's hand closed round the hilt of the knife behind his back.

'Ain't no call for that kinda talk, Jack. I don't know how you got such a loony idea in your head. I swear I don't.'

'What's that you've got behind your back, Henry?' Jack Almont asked with a quiet deadliness.

'I ain't got nothin' 'hind my back,' Scranton protested.

'Like I said, you're a low skunk liar, Henry.'

The moment which Henry Scranton figured was inevitable the second that Almont's instincts kicked in had come, and one of them had only seconds left to live.

★　★　★

Tod Lacey grumbled on feeling the prod of the rifle which Hank Carty was holding on him, thinking that it was downright unfair to be woken just as he'd found sleep. He rolled over and looked up at Carty standing over him, Winchester pointed and looking mighty sinister.

'On your way,' Carty ordered.

'Ain't hospitable to toss a man out in total darkness,' Lacey said.

'It ain't,' Carty admitted. 'But it would be a fool that would let you hang around a woman who ain't experienced in worldly ways, Lacey. So it's leave right now, or I'll plug you. Choice is yours.'

Lacey rubbed his stubbled chin. 'A choice like that ain't no choice at all, friend.'

'It's all that's on offer,' Carty stated tersely. 'If you leave, to sweeten the deal I'll give you a horse, throw a saddle in too. It's a good offer. That wormbait nag you've got will fold soon and leave you stranded.'

'You must want rid of me real bad.'

'Yeah. Real bad. What's it to be? Horse or bullet?'

'Lead poisoning ain't good for a fella's health. So horse it is.'

'Good choice,' Hank Carty said. 'We'll head over to the corral right now.'

'And there I was having sweet dreams.' Tod Lacey sighed. 'Am I allowed to stretch to get my back straight?' Lacey sat up and raised his hands above his head. 'That sure feels good. Let's go, then.'

Hank Carty let his guard down for a split second, but that was enough time for Lacey to swing his leg and take Carty's from under him. The rancher tumbled helplessly backwards.

★　★　★

Jack Almont had his six-gun almost clear of leather when he felt the burn of the knife Scranton had thrown in his belly. With the speed of a mountain cat,

Scranton was on him, ramming the blade deeper into Almont's innards. Almont could feel the knife slicing his organs, and the awful ripping of his gut when Scranton twisted the blade viciously. Finally, though by then it did not matter any, Jack Almont dropped to his knees, his face a mask of disbelief, reaching out to clutch at Scranton who stepped back contemptuously. Almont rolled on to his side and drew his legs up into a foetal position. His groan was ripped from his heart. Then he lay still, washed in moonlight, his face a mask of surprise.

★ ★ ★

Mounted up and ready to ride, Saul enquired, 'Where are we headed, Mr Tyrell?'

'The Carty place,' Tyrell answered.

'Kinda late for a social call, ain't it?'

'Stop your fool questions!' the owner of the Circle T barked. 'Ride!'

On hearing the rifle shot, Lucy Carty's heart leapt into her mouth. She jumped from bed and hurried along the hall to her pa's room. Finding it empty, her spirits hit the floor. Gunshot could only mean one thing.

Trouble with a capital T.

★ ★ ★

As he fell backwards Hank Carty triggered the Winchester. The bullet whizzed past the side of Tod Lacey's head and, luckily, nicked the top of his right ear, which probably deflected its trajectory the fraction of an inch that prevented it from boring a hole in his head. His shock had almost given the rancher time to set up a second shot that would have purposeful menace to it rather than accidental wildness. Lacey stamped on Carty's rifle hand.

'I mean you no harm, you damn fool!' he snarled. 'It's just that I take exception to being woken in the middle of the night and being prodded by a rifle. That kind of fool thing could make you wormbait in the blink of an eye.'

Carty relaxed. Lacey had talked sense. He'd have reacted in much the same manner were their positions reversed. Lacey grabbed the rifle.

'Now get up slow. Real slow,' Lacey cautioned.

'And you hand that 'Chester straight back to my pa,' Lucy Carty commanded from the open door of the barn. 'Or I'll drop you where you stand!'

'Ease off on the trigger, Lucy,' Carty ordered. 'It ain't what it seems.'

'It seems pretty straightforward to me, Pa,' Lucy said. 'You're on the ground and there's a man standing over you pointing a rifle.'

'Most of this was my doing, gal. Now do as I tell you!'

Tod Lacey offered his hand to help Carty up. When he accepted Tod Lacey's help, though puzzled, Lucy

Carty did as her pa had ordered.

'What the heck's going on here?' Lucy demanded to know.

Tod Lacey turned to face Lucy and instant shock registered on her face on seeing the copious stream of blood on his right cheek.

'My stray round clipped his ear,' Carty explained. 'Could've blown the top of your head off, so thank your lucky stars,' he told Lacey.

'Right now, it feels like it did,' Lacey threw back.

'Needs cleaning to avoid infection,' Carty said. 'Go boil water and get some clean rags,' he told Lucy. 'Git, gal,' he ordered, when Lucy remained rooted to the spot. 'Lacey and me will be along presently.'

★   ★   ★

His deed of Cain done, Henry Scranton put Almont back on his saddle and led his horse back along the trail to the southern boundary of the Carty spread, to put in place the last piece of Hank Carty's downfall. With Carty running off at the mouth, his neighbours would draw grit from his stand against Sam Tyrell and, as quick as a coyote could blink, the tide which was currently flowing in Tyrell's favour would turn. If that happened he'd be back on the trail scrounging a bed here and a meal there in the fashion that so many gunnies who were long in the tooth had to. He was determined that that was not going to be his fate. If his present plan worked in the way he figured it would, it would not be. He'd be sharing in Sam Tyrell's future as the Circle T reached ever wider boundaries.

7

Lucy Carty returned to the house twice as uneasy as she had been before. She could not, despite her best efforts, deny to herself that Tod Lacey had stirred a gnawing deep inside her that was both sweet in its pleasure and downright troubling in its persistence. And now, added to that, she had the worry of what might be brewing between her pa and Lacey. She knew that her pa still saw her as his little girl to be protected, and no matter how many times she reminded him that she was a grown woman more than capable of looking after herself, making up her own mind and making her own decisions, there was no changing his perception of her. 'There's men roaming in these parts who are worse than mangy dogs, Lucy,' he'd more than once reminded her. 'Men who would use a woman and

then toss her aside like an old boot.'
She had told him as many times as he
had reminded her that she could tell the
difference between a toerag and a good
man, but now she wasn't at all sure that
that was the case. Feeling the kind of
longing she was feeling for Tod Lacey, a
trail bum — probably the kind of man
that her pa had warned her about
— made her question her instincts,
though there was a softness in his eyes
that such a man should not have. Darn,
why hadn't Tod Lacey picked someone
else's henhouse to raid!

* * *

Henry Scranton drew rein and found
hiding just barely in time on hearing
the sound of riders approaching. From
the hollow where he had taken refuge
he watched Tyrell and two other riders
go past, and wondered what they were
up to. There was nowhere else to go at
the point they had reached on the trail
but the Carty place.

He dared not breathe when Tyrell's horse, picking up the scent of Jack Almont's blood, bucked wide-eyed.

'What's wrong, girl?' Tyrell calmed the mare to a degree, but there was no settling the mare fully. Tyrell's eyes searched his surroundings, looking for what had spooked the horse.

'Some night critter, boss,' Saul opined.

'I ain't too sure,' Tyrell said, intensifying his search of the trail.

'Ain't 'nother soul about, Mr Tyrell,' Larry said.

'I guess you're right,' Tyrell said after further consideration, and rode on.

Henry Scranton felt weak. Had Tyrell bothered to investigate just a little more, the cosy future he had planned for himself could have ended at the end of a rope. Allowing a goodly spell for Tyrell to distance himself, Scranton left the hollow and rode the short distance to the gully where he intended dumping Jack Almont's body.

★ ★ ★

'You had the upper hand just now,' Hank Carty said. 'You could have killed me easy, Lacey.'

'Why would I want to kill you, Carty?'

The rancher held Lacey's gaze. 'Don't take much for some men to kill another man.'

'Guess not.'

'Are you saying you ain't that kind of man?' Carty questioned.

'That's right. But I ain't making no claims to sainthood neither,' Lacey responded.

Hank Carty's smile was a broad one. 'Ain't many men in these parts, and I reckon most parts, who can claim sainthood. But there's a whole passel of territory between downright bad and downright saintly.'

Tod Lacey put his shoulder to the barn wall.

'Riddles tire a man's brain something awful,' he said. 'So if you've got something to say then say it, Carty. Or go back to bed, and I'll head out.'

'Where're you from, Lacey?'

'More darn questions. I just bet you get lots of headaches from asking questions.'

And why did you become a trail bum? 'Cause I reckon you weren't always one.'

'Don't much like that handle, mister,' Lacey said tetchily.

'Don't give a darn what you like and what you don't like,' Carty barked.

'Where I hail from don't matter. And why I took to travelling, I don't intend to tell you. And I don't give a darn whether you like or don't like that or not, friend.'

'Touchy critter, ain't ya.' Hank Carty held Tod Lacey's gaze. 'Sure you ain't a Tyrell agent?'

'Like I told you, I don't know any fella by the name of Tyrell.'

Carty yanked open the barn door. 'Let's go to the house.'

Lacey chuckled, 'You've got so many sides to you, you must confuse yourself, mister.'

Carty chuckled along with Lacey. 'It's been said.'

By now Hank Carty was of a mind to believe Lacey when he said that he did not know Sam Tyrell. But that did nothing to allay his fears about Lucy tying up with the stranger.

★ ★ ★

Henry Scranton reached the gully on the southern edge of the Carty place, where he dumped Almont's body. Then he went into the gully to place the item he had earlier stolen from the Carty house: the rancher's prized silver dollar, dented right in the centre where it had stopped a Reb bullet from ripping through his heart — Hank Carty's lucky piece. He placed the coin near to Jack Almont's body, but not in clear view. The silver dollar had to be found. If it was on show the finder might ask why, if he could see it, then why the heck hadn't Carty? The scene set, Scranton stepped back to examine his handiwork, and was well pleased with what he saw. He mounted up and rode back to the Circle T, confident that his future was rosy. It didn't trouble him any that, to secure that future, he had murdered one man in cold blood and had as good as done the same to the second man: Hank Carty. He doubted whether Tyrell would sling a rope for Carty (though he had not been rope shy before), because he was sweet on Lucy Carty, whom he saw as a fitting mother to the string of sons he planned on fathering to pass his legacy on to. 'There'll forever be a Tyrell in these parts,' was his boast. Now, unless he could arrange otherwise, and there was no obvious way that he could see that he could, the noose that would stretch Hank Carty's neck would have to be sanctioned by a jury. It worried Scranton that that would take time, and his past experience was that time could play a whole passel of tricks that could upset a man's best-laid plans.

8

Lucy Carty stopped her fretful pacing of the kitchen floor and rushed to the door when she heard footsteps approaching. She held a lamp aloft to light her pa's and Tod Lacey's path.

'That was a damn fool thing to do, Lucy,' her pa rebuked her. 'What if it was some evil-minded critter was comin' a-callin'. Standin' in the light the way you was, you'd make a fine target.'

'Sorry, Pa.' Although Lucy had not seen or lived through the lawless times which her pa had lived through, and the West had been tamed some by the coming of law and order, hit and miss though it was, it was still for the foolish and careless a dangerous land where death and mayhem were never far away. 'Wasn't thinking.'

Hank Carty softened his attitude. 'Well, no harm done this time.'

Lucy's relief that she was not to be rebuked further in the presence of Tod Lacey was immense. Being in her early twenties, she wasn't much more than a girl in age, but the quivery sort of feelings she'd been having since Lacey stepped into her life had made her a full-blooded woman, she reckoned.

'I've got coffee brewing,' she said, eagerly stepping aside to let her pa pass inside, falling in beside Tod Lacey to find out how it felt to walk alongside him. It felt a whole lot better than she had imagined in the hours since she had first found him in the henhouse.

Hank Carty made a pretence of not having noticed, but he had, and his concern about the effect Lacey was having on his daughter took a leap. He began to question the wisdom of having let the saddle bum remain anywhere near her. It was a delicate game of timing. Run him out now and it would only serve to make Tod Lacey all the more attractive to his smitten daughter. But let him hang around for too long, and he would run the risk of Lucy's infatuation becoming something much more serious. He was honest enough to admit to his own fear of losing Lucy, and spending the rest of his days, whatever number God had allotted him, alone. No other woman would ever match up to his late wife.

Some men loved many times, and some only loved once.

'Coffee, huh?' Hank Carty grunted. 'I reckon something stronger, don't you?' he enquired of Lacey.

Suddenly Tod Lacey was a man with a dilemma, one which he was quick to cover, but not before the wily Carty noted his fleeting uneasiness and the quick flick of his tongue over quivering lips.

'Silly me.' Lucy laughed and went to the kitchen dresser from which she took a bottle of whiskey, which Lacey's gaze fixed on.

'Coffee will do me fine, ma'am,' he

said. 'I find that whiskey chases away a man's sleep.'

'Coffee? Sure?' she asked.

'Yes,' Lacey answered, after the briefest hesitancy.

'Dang it, daughter,' Hank Carty exclaimed when Lucy poured a short measure of whiskey. 'I'm drinking whiskey, not washing out my mouth!'

She poured a little more, and rejected her pa's objections. 'Whiskey's the devil's tool to turn a man bad, Pa,' she said.

Carty laughed. 'Gets more and more like her ma every day,' he told Lacey.

'In that case Mrs Carty must have been one fine and good woman,' Tod Lacey replied, bringing a blush to Lucy's cheeks with his steady gaze.

'That she was,' Carty said sadly. 'That she was.' He gulped the whiskey down in one swallow.

'Maybe some apple pie to go with that, Mr Lacey?' Lucy asked, handing Tod Lacey a cup of steaming-hot coffee.

'Coffee's just fine,' he said.

As he took the proffered cup his hand touched Lucy's, causing her to draw back. The coffee cup crashed to the kitchen floor. Lucy leapt aside as the hot liquid splashed about, causing her to lose her balance, making it necessary for Lacey to grab hold of her. His movement brought Lucy and him close together, his arm round her waist. Her eyes locked with his. The entire episode lasted only seconds, but it was long enough for Hank Carty to come to a decision.

'I swear, I'm the most awkward creature ever assembled by God,' Lucy said, her laughter short and breathless. 'I'll pour you another cup, Mr Lacey.'

Lacey looked at Carty, instantly reading his mind. 'I reckon I'll just head back to the barn and bunk down,' he said. Lucy's disappointment could not be hidden. 'See you good folks in the morning.'

★ ★ ★

An hour passed before Hank Carty put in an appearance at the barn.

'I guess you know why I'm here, Lacey,' he said.

'I guess so.'

'That horse is saddled in the corral.'

Tod Lacey rolled out of his blanket and dusted off the straw he'd been lying on. Carty held out a fist of dollar bills. 'That should see you a goodly distance away.'

Lacey looked at the dollars, left Carty holding them, and walked past. 'Never took charity, ain't going to start now.'

'This ain't charity,' Carty barked. 'Let's call it . . . *stay away from my daughter* money, Lacey.'

'You can still keep it!'

'So be it. But if you've got any ideas about cosying up to Lucy, just keep in mind that a dead man can't do that.'

'You ain't got anything to worry about, Carty.'

'Good to hear that. But you just keep in mind what I told ya.'

'I ain't got a hankering to stay round here,' Lacey said. 'Figured I'd go south of the border for a spell.'

'Mexico, huh?' Carty grunted. There was a world of meaning in the rancher's tone. Mention of Mexico had confirmed his idea that Tod Lacey might be dodging the law. Lacey was not of a mind to contradict him. It didn't matter one way or the other what Carty thought of him, and he saw no point in wasting his breath trying to convince a man who had probably had his mind made up from when he first set eyes on him. 'Stick to what you say, and if the law comes by, I'll tell 'em you were here and headed north.'

'Thanks for the nag.'

'These dollars are still yours if you want 'em.'

'A horse I need, so I'm obliged to you for it. But I ain't going to take your money, Carty!'

Tod Lacey left. He was mounting up when he heard a bolt being slid home on the door. Angered, he swung the horse towards town. He had intended making tracks right away for the border, but now he decided to stay a couple of days in town to see if he could pick up a couple of dollars doing whatever work happened along.

★ ★ ★

Watching from a rise overlooking the Carty place, Sam Tyrell said to the riders with him, 'Now I wonder who that is? You boys hear that Carty had a visitor?'

Both men shook their heads.

'Whoever he is, he looks like a man I'd be slow to tangle with,' the man called Saul said.

'Sits a horse well, don't he,' Tyrell commented.

'Looks a handful all round to me,' Larry commented.

Sam Tyrell was not ready to admit it, even to himself, but on first sighting he'd much prefer to have the stranger on his payroll than on Hank Carty's side.

They drew back into the trees when Tod Lacey came along the trail to town, observing him close up.

'Dusty,' Larry said. 'Been on the trail a long time.'

'Kinda skinny, too, ain't he,' Saul added. 'Trail bum, I reckon.'

'Mebbe,' his partner said. 'But I reckon bummin' ain't been his style always.' Larry screwed up his eyes. 'Ya know, put a bit of beef on him and I think I seen him some place before.'

'Where?' Tyrell asked sharply.

'Can't rightly say, Mr Tyrell. But I guess it'll come to me.'

Sam Tyrell's enquiry had been sharp of tone because, like his hireling, he too had a sense of having seen the stranger somewhere before. And he was left with the impression that he was an *hombre* with a hard-as-nails disposition.

★ ★ ★

'Stop fussin' so, gal,' Hank Carty growled. 'And there's no need for a third place setting.' Lucy Carty came up short, spun round from the cooking stove and trapped her pa's eyes with a fierce look, knowing well what he was going to say before he said it. 'He's gone.'

'Up and left, huh?' she said with false airiness.

'No.'

Her look became even more fierce. 'You told him go?'

'It's for the best.'

'Whose best would that be, Pa?'

'I could see the hankering in ya for him, Lucy. Getting involved with a man like that — '

'What kind of a man would that be, Pa?' she challenged.

'The kind of man who'd probably leave you on the trail some place with a swollen belly. That kind of man! Or maybe sell you the other side of the Rio to a Mex whorehouse.'

'I'm twenty-three years old and can

make up my own mind, Pa!' She slammed down the plate of eggs and bacon she was holding on the table, shattering it. The food scattered across the table and on to the floor.

'I'll not abide shows of bad temper, Lucy,' Carty yelled. 'I'm your pa, and you'll do as you're told, you hear.'

'Oh, I hear good, Pa,' she chanted.

'Good.'

'But that don't mean I'm heeding.' She ripped off the gingham apron she was wearing and, throwing it on the floor, she headed for the door.

'And where do you think you're going?' Hank Carty demanded to know.

'To be married!'

'What? Talk sense, woman. Married, you say?'

'Married,' Lucy Carty stated resolutely. 'To Sam Tyrell.' Carty sat stock still, staring, as if turned to stone. 'He's asked me often enough. And now, if he'll have me, I'll be his wife.'

Hank Carty's mouth opened and closed like a fish out of water. The words he wanted to say were in his head, but there was no way that he could get them to his lips. When he eventually got his speech back, he groaned.

'What have I done?'

9

At first sight, in the grey dawn, the
town of Lucky Hollow did not make
much of an impression on Tod Lacey.
He reckoned that the longer he stayed
around the less favourable his opinion
would become. It was the kind of town
where a man needed to shake its dust
off as quickly as he could, before he lost
the will to make the effort to move on.
But moving on was nothing new to
him; he'd been moving on for a spell
now not knowing what he was looking
for, or even whether he'd recognize it
when he found it, if he ever did. He'd
never have figured himself to be a
wandering man, but had found that
once roots were pulled up, it became
increasingly difficult to put them back
down with each new town visited and
every new trail traversed. A man devel-
oped a wanderlust, especially when he

was running from his past.

The only company he had along the main drag was a mangy dog, recognizing another outcast from decent society. He checked the store windows for hiring notices and saw none. On reaching the saloon, the familar shakes that such an establishment brought on manifested themselves. His throat went suddenly dry and his mouth had the feel of sand in it. The fiery rawness spread into his belly, causing his innards to bunch together painfully. A sweat as cold as a dead man's touch oozed through his pores and bathed his body and face. The mangy dog whimpered and settled wide, lonely eyes on Lacey, understanding his pain, he felt.

He rode on. But he might not have, if the saloon had been open.

★　★　★

Sam Tyrell was woken by the helter-skelter arrival in the yard of a fast-ridden horse. He leaped out of bed and immediately buckled on his gunbelt over his nightshirt. A fast-ridden horse mostly meant trouble not far behind.

He hurried downstairs, collecting a shotgun from the den on his way. Nothing like a blaster as a persuader. There was a commotion outside. He yanked open the front door, shotgun primed, and poked its barrels in to Lucy Carty's shocked face. In a second flat he dropped the shotgun and became conscious of his attire. Lucy's laughter did not help.

'Do you still want to marry me, Sam Tyrell?' she asked, when she stopped laughing.

'M-m-mar . . . ?' he stammered, stunned and tongue-tied.

'It's a simple yes or no question,' Lucy stated clearly.

Gathering his wits, Tyrell gave a resounding 'Yes,' to Lucy's question, and added, 'Darn well, yes, woman!' At that moment Sam Tyrell had only one fear, and that was that he'd wake up. He grabbed hold of her and kissed her full on the mouth. He decided that he was not dreaming.

'Now you behave yourself, Sam Tyrell,' she rebuked him, shoving him away. 'Don't you be taking liberties, before liberties are your due.'

'You're going to be my wife, woman.'

'That's so. But you keep your distance until it's respectable to be in a clinch!'

'Ma'am,' he said. Then, frowning. 'What's your pa got to say about this?'

'I'm my own woman,' Lucy answered, her humour dogged. 'I make up my own mind. And put on your pants. Never figured you for the nightshirt type, Sam Tyrell.'

'Be right back,' he promised.

He went back inside the house, but on hearing hoofs Tyrell popped his head back out of the door in time to see Hank Carty charging into the yard, wearing a scowl that would put legs under the devil. He hit the ground running, and grabbed hold of Lucy, delivering a curt order.

'Back in the saddle, gal! I'll not tolerate any of your foolishness.'

'Woman,' Lucy corrected.

'For two bits I'd put you 'cross my knee, *gal*,' he stressed. 'Now do as your pa tells ya. And be quick about it.'

Sam Tyrell stepped on to the porch. 'If Lucy wants, she can stay right here where she is, Carty. Like she said, she's a woman now.'

'No burst of mule-headedness makes her a woman, Tyrell,' Carty growled. 'If she thinks you're a man, all she is, is a child with a wilfully stubborn streak. Just like her ma, rest her soul,' he added proudly. 'Back in the saddle, daughter.'

'She's as good as my wife, Carty,' Tyrell declared angrily. 'So leave her be.'

'Your wife?' Carty snorted.

'It's the way she wants it to be,' Tyrell said cockily. 'Rode in and asked me straight if I wanted her as my wife. I said yes. Tell him, Lucy.'

'Are you loco, gal!' Carty roared. 'You tied to a no-good,' his finger pointed at Tyrell, 'like him? He ain't nothing but a jumped-up toerag who came by his fine house and fancy duds by any means includin' murder, I reckon.'

'That, my friend — '

'I ain't your friend, Tyrell,' Carty flung back.

' — is a mighty big statement, which I hope you can prove. Or . . . ' Tyrell's tone dropped several notches, 'back up with spitting-iron, Carty.'

The moment he'd foolishly let his pride override his good sense, Tyrell knew that he'd overstepped the mark.

'Don't talk so to my pa,' Lucy protested.

'You're on my side now, Lucy,' Tyrell bellowed, figuring that bluster was all that was left to him to retrieve the situation.

'That's what this darn valley's come down to,' Lucy declared hotly. 'Sides! Why can't folk simply mind their own

109

business and let everyone else mind theirs?'

'It ain't as simple as that,' Hank Carty stated. 'Not when someone who blew in on a tumbleweed figures that he'll poke his nose into everyone else's affairs and grab the land they sweated blood on. Folk like your ma and me, gal!'

'I think the time's come for you to choose, Lucy,' Tyrell stated gruffly.

'That it has,' Hank Carty grunted.

Lucy Carty's eyes flashed between the pair. 'It shouldn't be that I'd have to choose between the man to be my husband and my pa,' she stated defiantly. Neither Tyrell or her pa gave ground. 'Well, the two of you can go to hell!'

'What?' they shouted simultaneously.

'You heard,' she said, and swung into the saddle.

'Where're you headed?' both men asked.

'Town.'

'Town,' both men yelped.

'To a rooming-house.'

'What for?' Carty enquired.

'Ain't that plain, Pa. To rid myself of two ornery critters who ain't got a pinch of sense between them.'

'Town's got real wild,' Carty said, his concern obvious.

'Maybe I'll get wild too, Pa. You know, I can warble a bit, and the saloon's looking for a warbler. So maybe Ike Bannion will hire me.'

'Ike Bannion sups with the devil,' Carty fumed. 'It ain't fitting to breathe the same air as Ike Bannion.'

'Well, it can't be as bad as trying to live with two men who think they own me lock stock and barrel. I don't aim to be owned by anyone, you hear, both of you?'

'Saloon warblers don't just warble,' Hank Carty said. 'They've got to . . . well, do other things, too, to earn their keep.'

'I know that. I wasn't found under the last head of cabbage, Pa.'

'I'll see you married to Tyrell before

working for Ike Bannion,' Carty stated grudgingly.

'Oh, I've changed my mind about marriage, Pa. I don't know what kind of loco bug got into me coming over here proposing marriage to a man like Sam Tyrell.'

'Is that so,' Tyrell growled.

'Darn, it would mean waking up each morning for the rest of my natural, lying next to a toad.'

Tyrell stepped down from the porch and grabbed the reins as Lucy was about to turn and ride out. 'Maybe I'll take you anyway, missy,' he threatened. 'As well as everything else in this valley.'

Hank Carty swung a haymaker, which the younger and more spritely Tyrell side-stepped. Carty's momentum took him past Tyrell, who placed a boot on his behind to send him sprawling on the dusty ground.

'Pa!'

Lucy sprang from the saddle and went to help her pa up. He shrugged off her help.

'I can get to my own feet, without the help of a skirt!' he growled.

The Tyrell men who had gathered to watch the three-way tussle burst into spontaneous laughter when Hank Carty had been dispatched to eat dirt. Some of the laughter was genuine, but mostly it was to please an employer who paid well and in whose employment they wished to remain.

'If I had a gun,' Carty foolishly challenged.

'Ain't no problem, Carty,' Tyrell growled. He pulled a six-gun from the holster of the man nearest to him and threw it at Hank Carty's feet. 'All you've got to do is pick it up.' Tyrell had decided to follow the course he'd mentioned only moments before. He'd eliminate his problem in the valley and take Lucy Carty whether she liked it or not. He needed sons to hand on his ill-gotten gains to, and sons he'd damn well have.

Hank Carty knew he'd overreached. The steely menace in Sam Tyrell's eyes rooted him to the spot. He had never seen Tyrell use a gun, but he had no doubt that a gun would fit his mitt like a well-tailored glove. Like his foe, he had let his pride get the better of his judgement. He was no gunslick. In fact a gun didn't even feel right in his hand. He did not know how fast Sam Tyrell was, but he figured that sleep-walking, he'd have the beating of him. The laughter had stopped, and men were edging aside to avoid stray lead.

'Stop this madness,' Lucy pleaded.

'Mr Tyrell's been called, ma'am,' said the man whose gun Tyrell had borrowed. 'Right's on his side.'

'Shut up, you snake in the grass!' Lucy exploded.

The man chuckled. 'Sticks and stones, ma'am. Sticks and stones.'

'More yellow in Carty than a daffodil's got, boss,' another man said.

Goaded, Hank Carty reached down and picked up the six-gun.

'Don't, Pa,' Lucy pleaded. 'You're no gunman. You don't stand a chance.' She turned to Tyrell. 'It'll be pure murder.'

Sam Tyrell pondered for a spell. When he spoke, his proposition had the whip of a lash on naked skin. 'Your ranch and your daughter for your life, Carty,' he stated.

Lucy Carty was stunned.

'What's it to be?' Tyrell prodded. 'Don't want to die of old age before you make up your mind.'

'In exchange for my life, I might trade my ranch,' Carty stated. 'But I'll die before I'll trade Lucy.'

Tyrell sighed. 'Then I guess you're going to die.'

'When this is finished with, Lucy, you find Tod Lacey and ask for his protection, gal,' Carty said.

'Lacey?'

'Yes,' Carty said impatiently. ''Cause I gotta feeling deep in my gut that he's got the whipping of Tyrell, and any man he's got on his payroll, too.'

Lucy was clearly on the horns of a dilemma. She reached a decision with sparkling clarity — the only decision that could be made. 'The last thing we need is another fast gun in this valley, Pa.' She stepped between Tyrell and Carty. 'I guess you're going to have to shoot through me, Tyrell,' she stated boldly.

10

'Ain't got any work right now, mister,' the livery owner told Tod Lacey. 'And I'm real short of oats right now, too,' he added in response to Lacey's request to purchase feed.

'A livery short of oats?' Lacey questioned sceptically.

'Waiting delivery,' Nat Clark said, not bothering to dress up his lie.

When he had turned into the livery a couple of minutes before, Lacey had not missed Clark's quick appraisal of the newcomer, and like his lie, he had done nothing to hide his opinion of Lacey either.

Saddle tramp!

'Got a monicker, mister?'

'Lacey. Tod Lacey. When do you expect a delivery of oats?' Clark shrugged. 'Ain't too keen on business are you, friend?'

'Maybe I'm particular who I do business with,' Clark replied. Nat Clark cast his gaze beyond Lacey to his horse and the brand on the mare's right-side hindquarters — HC. Lacey followed the livery owner's line of vision, and when he returned his gaze to Clark the livery owner had used the brief spell of inattention on Lacey's part to pick up the rifle that had been resting against a bale of hay a short distance from where Clark had been standing. 'That's Hank Carty's brand, mister.'

'It is,' Lacey confirmed. 'He gave me the horse.'

'Gave, huh?' Clark snorted. 'Hank's one to mind a dime. Some would even say that he's a skinflint. So why would he gift you, a complete stranger, a nag?'

'He had his reasons.'

'That a fact? And what would them reasons be?'

'None of your business, mister,' Tod Lacey said stiffly.

'Lippy sort, ain't ya.'

'Only when I'm prodded by a nose-poker.'

'Nose-poker, huh!' Anger flashed in the livery owner's eyes. 'Folk look out for folk 'round here. Now I don't believe for one second that Hank Carty parted with good horseflesh for free. I reckon that you're a lowdown horse-thief. And I also figger that you thieved that horse after you shot down Hank and probably Lucy Carty too, with that well-polished six-gun poking out of your saddle-bag.'

Tod Lacey cursed his carelessness.

'That's a mess of reckoning and figuring, friend — '

'Ain't your friend by a long shot,' Clark spat.

' — But you're as wrong as wrong can be.'

'Don't reckon I am,' Clark stated positively. 'And,' he used the barrel of the rifle as a pointer, 'I'm also guessin' that you took that rig in your saddle-bag from another dead man. 'Cause right there,' he concentrated the deadly pointer like a schoolmarm's finger might to draw attention to a flaw in homework, 'it's got the initials JB on the handle. Now I ain't no educated man, but I know that JB don't spell Tod Lacey.'

Lacey silently cursed his carelessness for a second time.

'Ah. Ah.' Nat Clark checked Lacey's next words. 'Ain't interested in no cock-and-bull yarn. I've had enough of them. No, sir. You and me is takin' a stroll 'cross Main to the sheriff's office.' His eyes glinted greedily. 'Gotta price on your head?'

'You're wasting your time,' Lacey barked. 'It's like I said, the nag was given free.'

'Hah! And I'm the Angel Gabriel hisself. Makes no diff'rence if you walk 'cross the street or I drag ya. Choice is yours, mister. 'Cause I figger that the dodger 'bout you says Dead or Alive.' He came several threatening steps closer to Lacey.

'Git.'

120

Tod Lacey turned and walked ahead of the livery owner, because he figured that Nat Clark had got an idea from what he'd just said, and was of a mind, if given the least excuse, to collect on DEAD.

★　★　★

'Stand aside, gal!' Hank Carty ordered Lucy. 'I ain't 'fraid of Tyrell.'

Lucy swung around and snapped, 'What did I do to deserve a pa so dumb.'

'You button your lip,' Carty flung back. 'Didn't your ma never tell you that you don't talk to your elders like that?'

'She told me plenty. But I reckon that she could tell me a mountain of stuff more than she did, and it would be no use in making sense of you, Pa. If I step aside, you'll have wings in a second flat. You simply ain't no match for Sam Tyrell.'

'Sometimes a broken-down old man

like your pa can get lucky,' one of Tyrell's hardcases sniggered.

'You shut your mouth!' Lucy barked.

'No one tells me to shut my mouth,' the man raged.

'I am,' Sam Tyrell bellowed. The man's angry eyes clashed with Tyrell's. 'Pick up what's owing you and ride,' he ordered.

Sullen-faced, the man said, 'I've had enough of this outfit anyway. Anyone else comin'?' No one was of a mind to join him. He strode off to the bunkhouse, then turned. Tyrell, anticipating his mood and his move, shot him between the eyes. 'Take your pa home and hammer some sense into his dumb skull,' he told Lucy Carty. 'But this is a once off,' he warned Hank Carty. 'You keep that in mind.' Tyrell turned and strode to the house.

'Thank you, Sam,' Lucy called after him.

'Don't kowtow to a snake like him!' Hank Carty ranted.

Lucy's heart missed several beats when Tyrell's step faltered, but he walked on.

'Don't you ever know when to keep your gob shut,' she berated Carty. 'Get in the saddle. *Now*,' she ordered when he hesitated.

'I swear you get more like your ma every day,' he flung back, but there was a warm smile on his lips. 'And that ain't all bad.'

Lucy mounted up.

'Let's go home, Pa.'

Henry Scranton, who had arrived late but had got the jist of what had happened, blocked their way. 'You might be able to sweet-talk Tyrell,' he told Lucy, ''cause he's sweet on you. But I'm a diff'rent kinda man,' he added menacingly.

Lucy Carty stared the gunslinger right in the eye.

'You ain't no man at all, Henry Scranton,' she said. 'Now get out of my way, before I run you down.'

Seething, Scranton stepped aside.

'Things in this valley ain't settled yet by a long shot,' he warned.

* * *

As in all small towns, crowds quickly congregated when there was a chance of excitement, and word of the livery owner marching a stranger across the main drag under the threat of a rifle raced through town with the alacrity of a gale-driven bushfire.

'Who the heck is he, Nat?' enquired a man coming out of one of the opening doors.

'My, don't he look dangerous, honey?' the woman who joined him said.

'Don't rightly know who he is,' was Clark's reply. 'Says his name is Tod Lacey, but he's sporting a gun with JB as a mark. And he's saddle trash, riding a horse that belongs to Hank Carty, which I figger Hank didn't part with willingly.'

'Looks kind of good-natured to be

that bad,' a rosy-cheeked woman opined.

'Thank you, ma'am,' Tod Lacey said.

'Welcome I'm sure,' she replied, settling the wisps of hair that had escaped from her tight bun.

'Only a widder for six weeks and she's already looking,' said the woman who accompanied the man who had questioned Clark. 'Always said that Mame Watson ain't even half-decent, honey.'

The man shifted uneasily, because only the night before he had verified his wife's claim, and hoped to further test its veracity in the near future. Mame Watson cast Tod Lacey a come-hither look. She was an optimist, because horse-thieving was a hanging offence.

Sheriff Ben Allwood, his attention caught by the growing commotion in the street, went to yank open the law office door. His face was a question mark — a question mark that turned to surprise on seeing the normally unnoticeable Nat Clark prodding a stranger with a rifle and ordering him to walk faster.

Allwood came to the edge of the boardwalk.

'What's all this about, Nat?' he enquired.

'Got a fella you need to talk to, Ben. Told me a yarn with more holes in it than the winter woollies I bought twenty years ago for my honeymoon. Bet you got a dodger on him.'

'Don't think so,' Allwood said. 'But I'll sure check. Best show the gent inside.'

As he passed inside, Sheriff Ben Allwood scratched his stubbled chin thoughtfully. 'Ain't there a town to run?' he said to the crowd pressing on Clark's coat-tails. 'Then get to running it. Set the rifle aside,' he ordered Nat Clark.

'Don't figure that's such a good idea, Ben,' the livery owner replied. 'Reckon this one could be a slippery customer.'

Allwood searched Lacey. 'Nothing hidden. And no iron on his hip, Nat.

Teased guns have a habit of going off. Set the rifle aside and put me in the know.'

'What we've got here is a horse-thief at best and a killer at worst, Ben,' Clark declared.

'Hanging charges,' said the sheriff of Lucky Hollow, his eyes searching Tod Lacey for signs of him being guilty as charged, but seeing none. 'Proof?' he requested of the livery owner.

'I reckon if we mosey along out to Hank Carty's place, we'll find all the proof we need, Sheriff,' Clark said. ''Cause he's riding a mare with Carty's brand. Says Carty gave him the nag freely.'

'He did,' Lacey said.

The lawman shared the livery owner's opinion of Hank Carty. Sheriff Ben Allwood looked steadily at Tod Lacey. 'Round these parts it's said that Hank Carty's got his first dime still, stranger.'

'I told him that,' Clark said.

'You got a tongue, mister,' Allwood asked Lacey.

'Does it matter if I have?'

'Don't get your drift.'

'I figure, why waste my breath, Sheriff? I'm a whisker away from a hang rope anyway.'

Ben Allwood reacted angrily.

'I don't sling a rope unless there's good reason to,' he barked. 'I wear a badge, and I wear it proud!'

'If that's so, it's to your credit.'

'It's so, stranger. Now you give me one good reason to not hang you, and quickly.'

'My story is true, Sheriff,' Tod Lacey restated.

'Well now, if that's so, then it's surely a turn up for the books. Hank being that generous.'

'Hogtie me, and let's ride out to the Carty ranch,' Lacey said. 'I ain't got any fears.'

Sheriff Ben Allwood said, 'That's a good offer. Let's just do that. What's your handle, stranger?'

'That's another thing,' Clark pounced, determined to see Lacey done for. 'Says

128

his monicker is Tod Lacey. Only he's got a gun in his saddle-bag with the initials JB on it. Now JB ain't the initials of Tod Lacey.'

'I can figure that, Nat,' Allwood said, sharp of tone. He squared up to Lacey. 'Well?'

'The gun's got nothing to do with this, Sheriff.'

'Is that so?'

'It is.'

'Tell you what, stranger. This is my town, and I'll decide what needs explaining. Understood?'

'The gun belonged to a friend.'

'Where's this friend now?'

'In someplace he don't want to be.'

'Hell?'

'I guess,' Lacey said.

'Tell you what. Let's make tracks for Carty's place for starters.'

'Fine with me.'

'I'll ride along with you,' Nat Clark told Allwood. 'And I'll bring a nice new rope.'

'You'll go back to forking hay, Nat,'

Allwood said. 'You're much too eager to sling rope to be on this jaunt.'

'He's my prize, Ben,' Clark protested.

'And you'll get credit if credit is your due,' the sheriff promised.

'You watch this *hombre* every second, Ben.'

'Every second,' the sheriff assured the livery owner.

★   ★   ★

Henry Scranton was a worried man. Tyrell had not enquired about Jack Almont, and he fretted that the Circle T boss would take it for granted that Almont, who had mouthed off a time or two about high-tailing it (not meaning a word of what he said) had done just that. And that was the last thing he wanted to happen, because it would scupper the easy-street life he had planned.

He needed Tyrell to find Jack Almont's body, and the planted evidence that would lead the hangman to

130

Hank Carty's door. He was figuring a way to do just that when luck favoured him.

'Hey, Scranton.' A man called Billy Scott hailed him from the far side of the yard. 'You seen Almont around?'

'Not since yesterday,' Scranton answered, in a tone he hoped sounded uninterested.

'The bastard owes me fifty dollars he lost at poker. Saw him ride out last night, figured he was on his way to town. But he ain't arrived back.'

'Funny thing. Mr Tyrell asked me to find him last night. Rode over to the Carty place, reckoned that Almont's hankering for Lucy Carty might have taken him that way, but it didn't.'

'Did you check in town?' Scott quizzed.

Scranton shook his head. 'It was late. If Jack had gone to town, I figured he'd have cosied up to a woman by then. So I came right back here. Why don't you ask Bart Halligan. He's been to town for supplies. He's over in the grub store.'

131

'Now why didn't I think of that?' Scott said, walking away scratching his head. Scranton hung about until Scott returned with the answer he already knew. 'Almont wasn't in town.'

'You go back to what you were doing, Billy. I'll find out if Mr Tyrell knows anything.'

'Mighty kind of you, Henry,' Scott said.

'No bother at all. And don't fret about that fifty dollars. Me and Jack Almont are real close. He wouldn't high-tail it without me along.'

'Guess not,' Scott said, relieved.

Thanking his lucky stars that Billy Scott had given him a reason to jaw with Tyrell about Almont, Henry Scranton hurried to the house.

11

'Hank Carty seems to be a popular fella round these parts, Sheriff,' Tod Lacey observed on leaving town under the hostile glare of the townsfolk who had gathered along the boardwalks.

'He's got his supporters,' Ben All-wood said. 'For tangling with a fella called Tyrell.'

'Sounds like you're one of them.'

'That's true enough. Ain't my kind of gent, Sam Tyrell.'

'Trouble brewing?'

'You're a real curious fella, ain't ya?'

'Interested, I would say, Sheriff.'

'There's a diff'rence?'

'I reckon.'

The lawman settled in his saddle and studied Lacey. 'You know, you've got a familiar cut to ya, mister.'

Lacey hunched his shoulders. 'Must be mixing me up with someone else.'

'Mebbe. But I'll keep you going round in my mind, Lacey.' Allwood had checked the dodgers before he'd left the law office and had found none for Lacey. 'That iron you had in your saddlebag. It's got the sheen of much use. Do you have an explanation for that?'

'It's an old belt I picked up in a card game.'

It was a lie.

'Is that so?' Allwood said quizzically, obviously not convinced. 'Nicely tooled belt. Expensive leather. Fancy craftwork, too. What was the name of this gent you parted from his rig?'

Tod Lacey snorted. 'You play poker, Sheriff?'

'I do.'

'Did you ever ask the fella you've just cleaned out his name?'

The lawman laughed easily. 'Can't say that it ever came up.'

'It ain't a natural time for small talk, is it?'

'No it ain't,' the sheriff of Lucky

134

Hollow agreed. He cast Lacey a sideways look. 'But at least we know that his initials are JB, don't we?'

'I ain't been around long,' Lacey said, feeling uneasy under Allwood's scrutiny, and with good reason. In the short time he'd known the lawman, he'd got the impression of a quick-witted and intelligent man, who'd put two and two together spit-quick. 'But it looks to me like you've got range war brewing?'

The lawman shook his head. 'Looked like that for a spell, sure enough, with Hank Carty and Sam Tyrell locking horns. But I reckon that most of the steam has evaporated.' He snorted. 'Carty talks loud. But Tyrell's money talks louder. I reckon that it's only a matter of time until Carty will have to do the same as everyone else in the valley, sell up to Tyrell.'

'This *hombre* Tyrell must be a well-bankrolled man, huh?'

'Ain't that a fact? Whatever he wants, he just buys,' Allwood said sourly.

'People. Stock. Range. Don't matter, he just buys.'

'People?' Lacey enquired meaningfully.

'Not the law, mister,' Allwood stated bluntly. His sigh was long and weary. 'Sam Tyrell's already bought the town. Soon he'll own the valley, too. And when he's got that in his pocket, he'll want to buy the darn county.'

Tod Lacey enquired with a keen interest, 'Where did this cash-rich fella hail from, Sheriff?'

'Ain't never said.'

'No one's ever asked?'

'A greased palm and free liquor seems to dull a man's curiosity, Lacey.'

'You never asked?' Lacey queried pointedly.

'Sure I did.'

'And?'

'And he told me he was from here and there.'

'You didn't pin him down?'

Ben Allwood drew rein. 'I've been the law in these parts for a long time, mister. I've risked fist, boot and shot in my time. Now I've got a coupla months to go to handing in my badge and buying a porch rocker. I figure that I've more than paid my dues, friend.'

When the sting had gone out of the liverish interlude, Allwood continued:

'Tyrell got off the stage a while ago, carrying a satchel full of cash.'

'How did he get his hands on all this money?'

'Not by foul means, it seems. I checked round. There was no bank, coach or train robbery that tied in with Tyrell's appearance here.'

'Tyrell might be the kind of patient *hombre* who'd lie low for a spell before he began to spend his ill-gotten gains,' Lacey speculated.

'Mentioned stocks and bonds a time or two.'

'Sound like you don't believe him, Sheriff.'

They had reached a long narrow draw on the most convenient route to Hank Carty's place. The two men had been riding alongside to that point but, with a careful distance between them, Ben Allwood now fell back. 'You ride ahead, Lacey,' he said.

Tod Lacey did as ordered.

'Oh . . . ' Tod Lacey turned in his saddle to look back at Allwood who now held a rifle across his chest. 'Turn in that saddle again before we clear this draw, and I'll drop ya, Lacey.'

'I ain't going to give you any trouble, Sheriff. No need to. Like I told you, the horse I'm riding, Carty freely gave.'

'Then you've got nothing to worry about,' said the sheriff of Lucky Hollow. 'Ride on. Nice and easy. Keep your pace steady.'

* * *

'What is it, Scranton?' Sam Tyrell growled, his sour mood of a while before having got even more sour. It was a mood Henry Scranton could understand. Lucy Carty was a woman any man would want to get into his

138

bed, and to be deprived of the opportunity just when he'd had it within his grasp would anger any man. He had been surprised by the patience Tyrell had shown; for himself, he doubted very much whether he could have been anyway near as tolerant of the shenanigans in the yard.

'It's about Jack Almont, boss,' Scranton said.

'What about him?' Tyrell asked vaguely, having something more urgent to ponder on.

'I didn't come across him last night. And he ain't turned up since.'

'Couldn't care less!'

Scranton held his panic in check. The last thing he wanted was for Tyrell to lose interest in Almont. If he did, he wouldn't bother to search for him. He took on a pose of deep concern.

'Spit it out, Scranton,' Tyrell commanded him.

'Well . . . ' Scranton held off elaborating to convey to Tyrell an impression of having difficult tidings to impart.

'Spit it out, I said. Or so help me I'll get a bullwhip and take the skin off your back, Scranton.'

'I didn't cross paths with Jack,' he said. 'But I did see sign near the Carty ranch . . . '

'And?' Tyrell prompted with blazing eyes.

'Well, just before he rode out, Almont was saying how he . . . he . . . '

'I'll cut your tongue out after I've skinned you alive, Scranton!'

'He talked about how he'd — '

'How he'd what?'

'Well, like to be the first man to . . . '

'To?' Tyrell growled, knowing well what Henry Scranton was trying to say if his tied tongue unfurled.

Having successfully conveyed that very idea by his hesitant rambling, Henry Scranton reckoned that if all else failed, he could take to the boards as an actor. Time now to put in the poison he'd been working up to. His expression was one of pain at having to betray a colleague and friend. 'I figger Almont was hangin' round the Carty place last night, Mr Tyrell. After you'd told ev'ry man jack not to go near the place.'

Sam Tyrell's fury reached into every corner of the room and beyond.

'I can understand how that would grieve you, boss,' Scranton said. 'You feelin' the way you do 'bout Lucy Carty. If Jack was sniffin' where he shouldn't been sniffin', you gotta right to whup him good.'

'Saddle the horses! Twenty men. Tell them to fan out and run Almont to ground.'

'Sure, Mr Tyrell. Are you ridin', boss?'

'Yeah,' Tyrell said grimly. 'I'm riding.'

'If you don't mind, I'd like to ride with you, sir.' Henry Scranton set his face in righteous stone. 'I warned Almont that if Lucy Carty was to be any man's in this neck of the woods, then that man would be you. So I'd like to be the man who'll hand out the punishment to Almont, if he's been foolin' round.'

Fooled by Henry Scranton's false show of loyalty, Tyrell said, 'You and me will do it together, Henry.'

'It'll be a pleasure I'll look forward to, Mr Tyrell, boss,' Scranton said, in the pious tone of a preacher man berating a sinner. 'I'll order up those nags right away.'

His treachery complete, Scranton left, much like Judas must have crept away after the betrayal of Christ, but having none of the regret and sorrow which Judas must have experienced. Henry Scranton had every intention of reaping the reward of his treachery without turning a single hair on his head.

* * *

Hank Carty dismounted and stormed to the house, the argument between him and Lucy about Tod Lacey, which had begun the moment they had cleared Tyrell's yard, still going as hot as hell's coals. Going inside the house, he yelled back the same answer he had given a hundred times along the trail.

'Lacey ain't fittin' for you. He's a damn saddle tramp. And no daughter of mine is going to hitch herself to no trail trash the likes of Tod Lacey!'

Lucy stormed in at the door behind him, her fury etched in every line of her face. 'Tod's no trail trash, Pa!'

'You know nothing of men,' Carty flung back. 'You leave picking a husband to me, gal.'

'I'll do my own picking, thank you very much, Pa,' Lucy flung back, her fury shooting up several notches.

'I don't understand you, daughter,' Carty yelped. 'One minute you're hauling me over hot coals 'cause I sent Lacey packing, next you're hauling me over those same hot coals by haring off to offer yourself to that no-good land-grabber Sam Tyrell.'

'I only went to Sam Tyrell, because I figure that to stop me marrying him you'd let me get tied to Tod Lacey as the lesser of two evils.'

Hank Carty's anger vanished. He chuckled. 'Got all of your ma's cunnin', too, gal.'

Lucy also relaxed. 'That's a real compliment, Pa,' she said softly. 'You miss Ma something awful, don't you?'

'The days have got a lot longer, and the nights a lot colder without her,' he said, his dewy-eyed gaze somewhere in a happier past.

A long way back, Lucy suspected.

Hank Carty snapped out of his reverie.

'Your ma left me holding a right feisty filly in you,' he said. 'Tod Lacey's gone, and best forgotten, gal.'

'I can't understand why he upped and left almost in the middle of the night, Pa,' she said sadly. 'That he didn't say goodbye really hurts.'

'Fellas of his ilk ain't the goodbye-saying kind, Lucy.'

'His ilk?'

'Yes.'

'Pa, you know what I reckon . . . '

'What d'ya reckon, daughter?'

'I reckon that Tod Lacey is no way near as black as you'd paint him. Sure, he might have fallen on hard times, no denying that. But I figure that though his outwards are saddle bum, his innards are gent.'

'Ah, you ain't thinking right, gal,' Carty said dismissively, but thinking on reflection that she might not be as far off the mark as he'd have her believe.

'I'm thinking clear as daylight, Pa,' Lucy Carty stated with sincerity. 'And right now I've got to put you on notice — '

'Notice? What kinda notice would that be?'

'If Tod Lacey ever breezes back this way, and he asks, wild horses won't keep me from riding alongside him over whatever trail he chooses to ride, Pa.'

Hank Carty was stunned by Lucy's sincerity and commitment to what she had stated. He wasn't a knee-bending man, but his praying started right then and there that Tod Lacey would keep riding the trail he'd chosen, and keep right on going.

His prayers were rejected.

'Riders coming in!'

Lucy Carty's announcement had Carty heading for the gunrack near the kitchen door, from which he selected a shotgun before opening the door, blaster cocked and pointed. The incoming riders were not those he expected to see.

'Howdy, Hank,' Ben Allwood hailed. 'No need for the blaster.'

Lucy Carty came to the door to join her pa and, on seeing who was riding with the sheriff of Lucky Hollow, her heart leaped into her mouth and her knees near buckled under her. 'Tod,' she murmured with a soft breathlessness.

'What can I do for you, Ben?' Carty enquired, as casually as his anxiety would permit.

'This feller here,' Allwood pointed, 'says that the nag he's on board was given freely. That so, Hank?'

Hank Carty had a dilemma he wouldn't wish on any man. An admission of the truth would alert Lucy to the fact that Lacey had not ridden out of his own accord, which could only mean that he had gotten rid of him to stymie her interest in him. Of course, she might think that if Lacey had accepted a pay-off he was no good anyway. But would it be wise, smitten as Lucy was, to bank on that?

After all, love was the blindest critter of all.

'That's his story, huh,' Carty grunted. 'Well it ain't mine, Sheriff,' he lied.

'You're saying you didn't give him that nag freely, Hank?'

'That's what I'm saying,' Carty stated tersely.

'That makes him a horse-thief,' Allwood said. Sensing an undercurrent that made him uneasy, he settled his gaze first on Lucy and then switched back to Carty, his stare fixed. 'Horse-thieving earns a noose round these parts, Hank.'

'I know what's what 'round here, Sheriff,' Carty barked, his eyes sliding away from Allwood's.

'What've you got to say now, feller?' Allwood enquired of Tod Lacey.

'The exact same as I said before. Carty gave me the nag freely.'

'That's calling me a liar!' Carty exploded.

Lucy Carty's heart missed several beats. She knew well what it meant when a man claimed he'd been called a liar, it gave him the right of challenge, and her pa was not a gun-handy man. 'Tod didn't say that, Pa,' she said.

Carty froze his daughter with the look one gives a back-stabber. 'No other conclusion can be drawn from what he said, gal!'

Lucy's face clouded with confusion. She was convinced that Tod Lacey was not a horse-thief, because if he was he could easily have raided the corral the previous night, and been gone before she arrived in the yard. However, she also knew that though her pa was a

148

gruff, even sometimes snarling man, folk who knew him and had dealings with him vouched for his honesty and truthfulness. 'Tod's no horse-thief!' The words were out before she knew her full thoughts.

'Nice of you to say so, ma'am,' Lacey said.

'If the saddle tramp is right, that makes me wrong, Lucy,' Carty snapped. 'Are you calling your own pa a liar, too?'

'I don't know what to believe any more, Pa,' Lucy said quietly. After she had studied both her pa and Tod Lacey she pleaded fearfully, 'My pa ain't gunslick, mister.'

'I ain't got a gun, Lucy,' Lacey replied. 'And even if I had, I wouldn't lean towards gunplay. Nothing good ever comes from it.'

'I'm the injured party,' Hank Carty said. 'I'll decide whether there's going to be gunplay or not, Lacey.'

★   ★   ★

The riders leaving the Tyrell yard fanned out in several different directions — their mission — to find and bring to book Jack Almont.

12

'Point your nag towards town, Lacey,' Ben Allwood directed, levelling the rifle he held on Tod Lacey. 'And you shut your gob, Hank,' he ordered, when Carty seemed of a mind to push for satisfaction. 'Lacey would kill you, you old fool.'

At this blunt statement Carty came up short.

'Now, I'll tell you what I'm going to do,' Allwood told Carty. 'I'll put this *hombre* behind bars for a cooling off period. So if you change your mind about anything, you drop by the law office in the next day or so, Hank.'

'If you're asking me, that's mighty generous treatment for a horse-thief, Sheriff.'

'I ain't asking,' Allwood replied sternly. 'Lead off, fella,' he ordered Tod Lacey.

Tod Lacey's denial of her pa's claim rang in Lucy's ears with the clarity of authenticity. Or was that just the way her ears heard it? Her heart had been beating an uncertain tattoo since she had set eyes on him again. Two things were certain: that one of these men she cherished dearly, and the other one who she reckoned had stolen her heart, was a downright liar. And no matter how the cards fell, when the truth eventually came out it would be a bitter pill for her to swallow.

'I'll round up a jury — '

'A jury?' Carty questioned Allwood.

'That's what I said,' the sheriff confirmed. 'The day for stringing a man up from the nearest tree is over. Law is coming to the territory, and I aim to see that it's upheld. So if a jury says that Lacey's offence is a hanging offence, then a gallows it will be. And if that same jury says that he ain't guilty by reason of argument, then he'll walk away a free man.'

'I should be walking right now,

Sheriff,' Tod Lacey said.

'If that's so, that means Hank is a skunk of a liar. Now why would he want to see you swing for something you didn't do, Lacey?'

Hank Carty worriedly watched Tod Lacey closely for his reaction and possible answer to the lawman's question.

Lacey knew that the answer that would explain why Carty had been so generous would only send a knife deep into Lucy's heart when she found out that he'd been bought off to high-tail it away from her, an offer he now deeply regretted having accepted. And the other side of the coin was finding out that her pa was prepared to send an innocent man to the gallows for his own ends. Either way there was a whole lot of grief for Lucy to bear. He could understand Hank Carty's desire to put distance between a saddle tramp and Lucy; postions reversed, he could not be sure that he wouldn't do the same. All he could hope for was that somehow he'd get the opportunity to escape and run for the border, a wanted man, but out of Lucy Carty's life and the damnation of Hank Carty's soul.

'I'm waiting for that explanation,' Allwood pressed Lacey.

'Let's make tracks for town, Sheriff,' he said.

'Not so fast,' Allwood said.

'Only doing what you told me to do, Sheriff,' Lacey argued.

'I've changed my mind. The situation is a mite diff'rent now, in that on the ride out here you were a man under suspicion. Now you're a prisoner with nothing to lose, Lacey. So that means I'll have to get my deputy out here.'

He turned to Carty.

'Hank, will you ride into town and bring Ed Furness back here?'

Obviously the lawman's proposition gave Carty a dilemma, which confused Lucy, who could not understand her pa's reluctance to comply with the sheriff's straightforward request.

For Carty, his fear was that leaving Lucy and Lacey in the same neck of the woods could prove too risky. Ben Allwood was an agile man in mind, though no longer in body. Tod Lacey would have the wily cunning of trail trash and was at least twenty years younger. He had probably been in a similar situation to the one he was now in a hundred times and more, and the proof of his cunning was evident in the fact that he was still sucking air and had not become wormbait.

'What're you waiting for, Hank? Get going. I want this *hombre* behind bars before nightfall.'

'With me gone, you'll be all on your own, Ben,' Carty fretted.

'I'll have Lucy to keep me company.'

That was part of what was worrying him. Lacey might overcome Allwood on his own. Or, smitten as she obviously was, judging by the flush of her cheeks and the lightness of her step on seeing Lacey again, Lucy might become party to helping Lacey. She wouldn't be the first woman in love who'd lost her senses. By the time he could get back from town with Ed Furness, she could be long gone with Lacey. 'That ain't no comfort,' he said in answer to Allwood. ''Cause if Lacey tricks you, it'll mean she'll be at his mercy.'

'I've got his measure, Hank,' Allwood growled, obviously taking umbrage at the doubt Carty's remark cast on his ability.

'I don't mean any slur,' Carty hurriedly assured the lawman. 'It's just that Lacey's trail wise. I bet in his time he's got the drop on a whole pile of fellas who thought they had his measure. What if I keep him covered and you head for town, Ben?' he proposed by way of compromise.

'Lacey's my prisoner. I'd have no right to turn him over to you, Hank.'

'You fellas seem to have a problem past fixing, gents,' Lacey said.

'I'll go,' Lucy said reluctantly, because the last thing she wanted was to see Tod Lacey behind bars, or her pa having a heart attack from fretting.

'No!'

156

'Someone's got to go, Pa.'

'How about me riding into town to bring back the deputy?' Lacey snorted.

'You ain't in no position to be sassy!' Lucy said. 'So hold your smart-alec tongue!'

'Ma'am,' Lacey intoned.

'And I ain't a ma'am. Not yet.'

'I've got an idea,' Hank Carty piped up.

'Hope it's better than your ideas so far,' Ben Allwood groused.

'Let's go together.'

'Having a woman tag along wouldn't be a good idea, Hank,' Allwood cautioned.

'I can take care of myself, Sheriff,' Lucy boasted.

'Well, I ain't going and leaving Lucy behind,' Carty said. 'You ain't keen on leaving Lacey behind, Sheriff. And I ain't going to leave Lucy on her own with a passel of Tyrell snakes in the grass.'

'Don't leave much choice,' Allwood grumbled.

'None at all,' Hank Carty said. 'I'll saddle a couple of horses right now. We should be in town before darkness comes.'

'Ain't I a privileged *hombre*,' Tod Lacey scoffed.

'Keep mouthing off and you could be as dead as you are privileged,' Carty flung back.

Tod Lacey's eyes met Lucy Carty's, and he was saddened by their dewy blue. He sighed wearily, thinking of another woman, and felt a mite guilty too that her memory should be tainted by thoughts of Lucy Carty.

* * *

Henry Scranton made a show of searching high and low, always getting closer to where he wanted to lead Sam Tyrell. As he got near to the place where he had dumped Jack Almont's body, he was careful to not be the one who found it, in a way that might start Tyrell thinking. He had seen evidence of his canny ways in the months he'd ridden for the Circle T, and he had come to the conclusion that the now eminently succesful and respectable rancher had not always been what he had become. Scranton reckoned that a look into Tyrell's past would dig up a pile of dark and dirty secrets. That was something to think about for the future; any such secrets could provide the means to muscle in even more lucratively than he was already planning to do.

But for now, there was the little matter of finding Jack Almont's body.

'Ain't nothin' 'round here,' Scranton called out, swinging off in another direction that would take the searchers away from the gully where Almont's body was. However, making an excuse of a need to relieve himself, he dismounted and went to the edge of the gully to do so. Suddenly he became agog. 'I'll be . . . ' He peered into the gully.

'What is it?' Tyrell asked.

Scranton scrambled down into the

gully and dragged Almont's body into the open before anyone else reacted. 'When I was sprayin' the daisies, I spotted a boot stickin' out,' he lied, when Tyrell and his fellow riders joined him. Then he held his breath. Someone else had to find Hank Carty's lucky piece. Sam Tyrell was no fool. Engaging in a pretence of thoughtfulness, Scranton wandered closer to where he had placed Hank Carty's silver dollar.

The ploy worked.

'Hey, lookee here,' a man shouted and bent down, inches away from Henry Scranton's toecap. 'Carty's the lowdown skunk who done for Jack Almont,' he said, holding out Carty's lucky silver piece in the palm of his hand for inspection.

'Let's ride,' was the chorus that went up.

Sam Tyrell held back for a moment to set his thoughts straight. Stringing up Hank Carty, attractive an idea as that was, would finish any chance of Lucy Carty having anything to do with him. But then, on the other hand, could Lucy manage alone, with Carty out of the way as her protector and a ranch that would need tending? Then there was the matter of the capital which he had prevailed upon the president of the Lucky Hollow bank to withold in order to force Carty in to selling up. Lucy's problems would mount fast and marriage to him, though not to her liking, if managed well, would quickly become the only option open to her. Of course there would be other men as anxious as he to offer Lucy Carty shelter, protection and sustenance, but those who would not be of a mind to have their palms greased to bow out, Henry Scranton and the Circle T hardcases, he was confident, could put legs under.

Made uneasy by Tyrell's hesitancy, Scranton (aware of Tyrell's continual intrigue where Hank Carty was concerned, to get his daughter into his bed, became fearful that at this late stage his well-planned scheme might come to nothing), enquired edgily, 'You ain't gonna let Carty get away with plain murder, are you, Mr Tyrell?' When Tyrell remained thoughtful, he added boldly, 'If nothin's done 'bout this, every rancher in the valley will read it as a sign of weakness, and they'll reckon that pushed, you'll crumble, boss.'

Scranton had to steel every nerve in his body to withstand Tyrell's fierce look. The other riders were divided between admiration for Scranton's outspokenness, and awe at his stupidity. In their experience Sam Tyrell was not a man to buck — or at least had not been in the past.

The seconds before Tyrell spoke were hellish for Henry Scranton. Tyrell had shown himself on occasion to be a man capable of firecracker anger. Driven by desperation, Scranton had gambled on boldness.

And it looked like he'd lost!

13

'Ease back, gal!' Hank Carty bellowed, when Lucy drew steadily level with Tod Lacey on their journey to town. 'If I have to use this rifle I'm holding, I don't want you in the way to catch lead.'

Lucy glanced back defiantly at her pa.

'Makes sense, Lucy,' Ben Allwood intervened, to stave off an impending bad-tempered dispute.

Not liking it any, Lucy Carty did as her pa had ordered, admitting to herself that he had indeed made sense, but only if Tod Lacey made a break for it, and she reckoned that he was not planning on doing so. Her assessment was based on her feeling that, had he wanted to, Tod, as she now thought of him, would have little difficulty in outwitting Allwood and her pa combined. She was of a mind to make her views known to both men, but better sense prevailed. There was no point in stirring more trouble; of that there was plenty.

They rode on in sullen silence. Dark storm clouds rolled in across the valley to match the mood of the party. Tod Lacey looked to the darkening sky, and was reminded of an evil day a couple of years before in a town called Haley's Ridge. Normally a busy trading town, Haley's Ridge was always a bustling place. However, on recollection, on that day it had had a brooding atmosphere that had seemed like a harbinger of doom to come; a harbinger that, in his delight of the news he had got from Doc Sommers shortly before, he had for once misread.

* ★ *

'I reckon, based on its mulish kick, that it will be a boy,' had been Sommers' prediction, having completed his examination of Sarah Barrow. 'And judging

164

by his feistiness, every inch as stubborn a cuss as his father, too,' Doc Sommers had joked. Barrow was Tod Lacey's real name.

He and Sarah had left Doc Sommers on wings, both of them grinning like kids with candy. Six years married, Sarah had given up on ever conceiving, therefore her joy was all the more ecstatic when Sommers had confirmed the pregancy eight months previously; a joy that had grown over the days and weeks since, until on this day Sarah glowed radiantly with an inner joy.

'John will be a doctor, I reckon,' she said proudly.

'John?' Marshal Jeff Barrow had questioned playfully, having not the least intention of contradicting his beloved spouse.

'Yes. John,' she stated uncompromisingly.

'Never said otherwise, wife.'

'And you'd better not, too, husband,' she said, hugging him to her.

'A doctor, huh?'

'A doctor, I said.'

'Not a badge-toter like his pa?'

'An honourable job, if done honestly as you have done it, honey,' Sarah said. 'But we've got to think ahead. Because by the time John's grown up, law and order will have come and badge-toters,' she grinned impishly, freckled nose puckered up, 'will have taken up knitting.'

They had laughed together, their joy utter and complete.

'I'll mosey along to the bank now, husband,' Sarah said.

They were passing the marshal's office when Willie Benn, his deputy, came to the door. 'Might want to see this, Jeff,' he said, holding up the telegram that the clerk had just delivered.

'You follow on,' Sarah said, when Jeff hesitated.

'What's it say, Ben?' he said, grudgingly.

The deputy handed over the one-line telegram which read:

BATEMAN OUTFIT IN YOUR NECK OF
THE WOODS.
SIGNED: JACK BATTLE US MARSHAL.

'Tough outfit, Jeff,' Willie Benn observed. 'A second wire says that Battle and two deputies will reach town in a couple of days.'

'Better make things ready, Willie,' Barrow said. 'Just in case the Bateman gang turns up here. Make sure we've got plenty of ammo. Try and swear in another couple of deputies. And let the business people in town know, so that they can check on their security. I'm on my way to the bank, so I'll let the bank president know of a possible threat.

'Heard tell that Ike Bateman's got this funny left eyebrow. A bullet creased it, took most of the brow and a deal of flesh with it, giving his left eye an oddish look that makes him recognizable.'

'Saw you and Sarah leave Doc Sommers,' the deputy said. 'Good news I hope.'

'The very best,' Jeff confirmed.

'Pleased for you and Sarah, Jeff.'

'Thanks, Willie. Be back in a little while. Meanwhile you keep a keen eye on strangers arriving in town.'

Jeff had only gone a few paces along the boardwalk towards the bank when two masked men burst out of it, six-guns blasting. A man about to enter was gunned down. Another, trying to regain his saddle suffered the same cruel fate.

Concerned about Sarah's safety, Jeff had frozen for a second and had lost the chance to surprise the bank robbers: the Bateman gang, no doubt. The third man coming from the bank, sporting a curiously odd left eyebrow, froze the very blood in his veins, because he was using Sarah as a human shield. 'Anyone feeling gun-happy, think again,' Ike Bateman yelled. He looked along the boardwalk. 'Got yourself a fine woman, Marshal.' Bateman's statement was evidence that he had been hanging around longer than the couple of minutes it had taken to rob the bank. 'Me and the boys might just take her along with us for some fun and games.'

Ike Bateman backed away to the horse another gang member held ready for him.

'Up you go, sister,' he ordered Sarah.

'Don't anyone do anything to risk Sarah's life,' Jeff had hollered.

'Sensible fella,' said Bateman. 'Now, just to be on the safe side, unbuckle your gunbelt, Marshal.'

'Ev'ryone do the same,' a second gang member called out.

'Do it!' Jeff shouted when one or two men hesitated.

A stray dog outside the hardware store knocked over a stack of buckets and they clattered on to the street. Unnerved, Ike Bateman swung around. His hold on Sarah loosened and she broke free of his grasp. Bateman's anger was white-hot. He shot Sarah in the back. Stricken, she looked at Jeff, reached out to him, smiled, and then sank to the ground.

Their ace in the hole gone, Bateman leaped into the saddle. 'Let's ride!'

The thunder of guns exploded over the town, but to no avail. The bank robbers, well versed in escaping flying lead, cut a path along the main drag, expertly bringing down a couple more of its citizens as they left town helter-skelter.

Jeff ran to where Sarah lay stricken, her smile sad, her eyes weary. 'Oh, hon, it hurts so bad,' she whispered when he took her in his arms. She gripped his hands in hers with her last ounce of strength. 'Don't you go all bitter now, Jeff,' she murmured. 'You hear?'

Her eyes rolled. Her smile became fixed. Her weary sigh was the gasp of death. Jeff Barrow's scream of anguish rose above the town like a banshee's, and followed the Bateman gang into the desert country beyond.

Willie Benn and several townsmen were already thundering past in hot pursuit of the Bateman gang. Within hours they had accounted for two of the Bateman gang, but not Bateman himself; he had been wily enough to slip away in the night to leave his fellow gang members penniless and trapped.

Ike Bateman had also taken the precaution of emptying their guns before high-tailing it, so that when the posse showed up, they were certain to be dead men.

In the weeks that followed Jeff Barrow spent more time in the saloon than anywhere else, until one day, waking to find his face in dogshit, he mounted up and rode away, reckoning that being a saddle tramp had more dignity than lying with dogshit on his face in the town he had brought ordered society to.

★   ★   ★

Lucy Carty wondered what sadness was causing Tod Lacey's shoulders to droop. She wished with all her heart, a heart that ached, that whatever terrible burden he was carrying she could lift it from him, or at least share in it with him. But that would never happen now. He was on his way to jail, and there was little doubt that her pa's word would have him convicted as a horse-thief. She knew well the kind of sentence that was handed down on such a conviction. She felt in the deepest part of her that Tod Lacey was not the kind of man he'd been painted. She sensed that he was a good man; fallen on hard times most assuredly, but that would not make him a bad man. However, there was her pa's word. She had never, neither had anyone else, ever known him to lie. He had always resolutely spoken the truth, even when it was to his disadvantage. Hank Carty had a reputation for truth and straight dealing. So why, to add to her woes, was she now doubting his utterances against Tod Lacey?

★ ★ ★

'What're we waitin' for,' one of the Tyrell riders demanded to know. 'Let's go and get Carty!'

Henry Scranton, had an uncanny knack of second-guessing another man's thoughts, a trick that had kept him above ground so far, served him well now. If he played his cards right he could make his future even more secure. He said, 'You fellas jerk rein for a bit, while me and Mr Tyrell jaw.'

Suspicious looks were exchanged all round.

'Do as he says,' Tyrell commanded, sensing that Scranton knew of his hellish dilemma and had a solution to it. Scranton rode off along the trail out of hearing. Tyrell joined him, enquiring: 'What've you got in mind, Scranton?'

'Well, I figure that stringing Carty up for all to see could bring a passel of trouble that even you couldn't handle, Mr Tyrell,' he said. Then he added with a wry, colluding smile, 'Sam.'

Tyrell's eyes narrowed in anger at the familiarity. But being a pragmatic man, he knew that he was over a barrel; there would be time later to deal with Scranton.

'I'm listening, Henry,' he said, matching Scranton's smile and manner — conspirators plotting.

'The way I read this,' Scranton began, 'is that you want Lucy Carty in your bed, Sam . . . '

'Never denied that I do, Henry.'

'But the danger is, that ain't goin' to happen if you string up her pa, Sam.'

'Wouldn't deny that either, Henry.'

'So what I'm proposing is, that instead of having Carty dangle on a noose for Almont's murder, you allow me to tend to matters in a way that no finger can be pointed at you or me. In fact, Lucy Carty won't see anyone's hand in her pa's demise except the hand of fate, Sam. After that the valley will be yours for the takin', and you'll comfort Hank Carty's grieving daughter right into the marriage bed, Sam.'

'You're a clever fella, Henry,' Tyrell said. 'So I figure for all of this helping hand stuff, you'll have something in return in mind?'

'I ain't gettin' no younger, Sam. I don't sleep too well at night on the trail no more. Bones begin to ache. Muscles tighten somethin' awful. And dreams ain't so pleasant no more — '

'Stop your rambling and spit it out, Scranton!' Tyrell barked sourly, his pretence of comradeship firmly ditched.

'Well.' Confident that he'd won himself a deal, Henry Scranton clapped himself on the back. 'I'd like to put down roots — '

'I'm getting dizzy going round bushes, Scranton,' Tyrell interjected, his mood even more sour. He vowed silently that at the first opportunity Scranton would pay with his hide for his duplicity, for he was now certain that Almont's murder was Scranton's doing, Scranton having murdered his former partner to engineer a deal that would end his trail days and save him from ending up in the gutter of some two-bit town, the smoke still drifting from the gun of the man who had outdrawn him.

'A coupla hundred acres in all this valley ain't too high a price for services rendered, I reckon,' Scranton said. 'And, of course, with all that grass I'm goin' to need cattle to chew on it too.'

'A high price,' Tyrell said.

'Don't figure it is, Sam.'

'Don't call me Sam, you two-faced bastard!'

'That's the deal,' Scranton snarled, gloves off. 'Carty out of your side as a thorn. And his daughter in your bed.' He snorted. 'If our positions was reversed, I'd grab it with both hands, Tyrell.'

'And if I don't agree?'

'I'll high-tail it.'

'After all this brainwork?' Tyrell said sceptically.

'But not before I get word out 'bout your plans to own ev'rything round these parts by fair means or foul, and there's already a lot of foul and no fair . . . Sam,' he added sarcastically.

'I could have you strung up right here and now, Scranton,' Tyrell boasted.

'Sure you could, Tyrell. But I reckon that would start talk, and talk brings questions. Have you got all the answers?' Henry Scranton stretched himself. 'Don't figger you have, Mr Tyrell. Give that fine upstanding lawman Ben Allwood the ghost of a chance, and you'll end up at the end of a rope or doin' a whole pile of hard time.'

He paused, grinning cockily and holding Tyrell's gaze.

'Ike Bateman.' He chuckled. 'Don't look so surprised, I know the fella whose bullet gave you that funny left eyebrow.'

After a long tense and angry interval, Tyrell asked, 'How're you figuring on giving Hank Carty wings?'

'There's that section of trail over the hills 'hind his place. The old outlaw trail to the border. In pretty bad shape. I figure that a man riding it could easily topple off into that ravine it circles.'

'What would Carty be supposed to be doing riding it in the first place?'

Henry Scranton shrugged. 'Only Carty would have known that. And he won't be able to say.'

Tyrell pondered for a spell, before saying, 'I'll take the boys back to the ranch. Be hearing from you.'

'Surely will. And . . . '

'And?'

'Tomorrow we'll settle those acres.'

'Sure. Best rejoin the rest. They must be quite curious by now.' Tyrell waved Scranton ahead.

'I'd prefer to let you ride ahead, if you don't mind, Sam. I've seen too many men shot in the back.' Scranton laughed. 'Too many to trust a man in a bind, Bateman.'

Sam Tyrell, now revealed as Ike Bateman, spurred his horse. 'All back to the ranch,' he ordered as he rode past the bewildered men.

'How 'bout Hen — ?'

The man who was about to ask the question as to why Scranton was taking

178

a different direction, had a friendly hand clapped over his mouth. The friend said, 'Don't you know enough not to ask stupid questions, Al?'

With the dust of the departing riders settling, Henry Scranton grinned and said, 'Guess it's time to secure that nest egg of yours, Henry.'

14

Hank Carty averted his eyes from his daughter's searching gaze.

'Have you got something you want to tell me, Pa?' she enquired, falling in alongside him.

'Tell you?' he grumbled, still not able to meet her eyes. 'Like what, gal?'

'I don't know. But you've sure got a sheepish look about you.'

'I ain't got nothing to tell ya!'

'It's time for plain talking, Pa,' Lucy Carty said, her mood uncompromising. 'I think you've lied about Tod Lacey — '

'Ain't so,' Carty barked.

Sheriff Ben Allwood turned in his saddle, surprised by the acrimonious tone of the exchanges between Hank Carty and his daughter. Everyone in the valley and further afield knew the respect and love in which Lucy Carty held her pa, and his respect and love for her was no less in return.

Conscious of his barked response to Lucy's quizzing, Carty's eyes clashed furiously with Allwood's but, as with Lucy's, they slid away to look at his surroundings as if he had never before seen the country they were passing through.

Now that she had bucked her pa Lucy, determined, readied herself to continue her challenge, but Ben Allwood beat her to the punch. The lawman drew rein. 'I've been mulling over what you said, too, Hank,' he said. 'And how shifty you've been acting since you said it.'

Hank Carty snorted dismissively.

'False witness will damn your soul to hell,' Allwood warned. 'And I reckon that will mean that you won't meet up with your wife again.' Hank Carty's eyes flashed alarm. ''Cause I ain't got a shred of doubt that Martha's with the angels, Hank.'

'I . . . I . . . ' His look at Lucy was one of desperation, but his attitude hardened. 'I ain't lied!'

'Then I guess we'll be building a gallows for Mr Lacey.'

Allwood swung his horse and pointed the mare in the direction of Lucky Hollow.

'Wait!'

The lawman swung back. Lucy stiffened in her saddle with expectation. 'I'm listening, Hank,' Allwood encouraged.

The seconds dragged on as Hank Carty dithered between truth and continued deception.

'Whatever you've said or say now,' Lucy said, 'you're still my pa, and nothing will ever change that.'

'I lied,' Carty blurted out. 'What Lacey's got of mine, he's been given freely.' He went on apace: 'You were all set to ride away with Lacey, gal. I couldn't let that happen. Throw yourself away on a saddle tramp. And besides, I'd surely be dead in a week without you around.'

'Oh, Pa.' Lucy wept. She leaned over

and hugged her father. 'Some day I'll have to find me a husband, you know that.'

'Not Tyrell or,' he pointed an accusatory finger at Tod Lacey, 'him!'

'No, not Sam Tyrell.' Lucy looked at Lacey. 'But I'm not so sure that Tod's the bad lot you're making him out to be, Pa.'

Hank Carty looked long and hard, first at his daughter, and then at Tod Lacey. 'Mebbe, gal,' he conceded. 'Mebbe.'

'Does this mean I'm free to ride on, Sheriff?' Jeff Barrow asked.

Ride on. The words burned holes in Lucy Carty's heart. The irony of the whole thing was that the revelation of the truth, due to her probing, had only brought about the same outcome as her pa's deception had been intended to: that was to rid her of the man she knew as Tod Lacey.

Her anger was sudden and hot. Maybe Tod Lacey was better gone, if he had no gratitude for her having saved his neck from a hangman's rope!

Ben Allwood considered for a moment. 'You will be, as soon as I check my dodgers back at the law office,' he answered in reply to Lacey's question.

'You've already checked, Sheriff.'

Allwood's scrutiny of Lacey was close. 'I still reckon I've seen you before some place, fella. So I figure giving you bed and board overnight might give me time to nail you down.'

Tod Lacey sensed eyes watching. He let his gaze wander over the country near at hand; he could see no one, but then the watcher would have been careful not to be seen, because if he had hidden himself away his intentions were malign.

'Take the lead to town, Lacey,' Allwood said. 'And no sudden moves.'

'Mind if I ride along?'

'I do,' Hank Carty replied in answered to Lucy's question to Allwood. 'This is deadly country in full daylight. By the time you'd be coming home it would be dusk at least, if not outright night.'

'I'll overnight in town with Mrs Reilly, Pa.'

'A boarding-house costs.'

'I'll work off my debt by making breakfast. Getting arthritic as she is, Mrs Reilly will welcome the help, I reckon.'

A boarder at Reilly's, Ben Allwood said, 'I could do with a good breakfast, Hank.'

'In that case I'm making you personally responsible for Lucy's safety, Ben.'

Lucy kissed Carty on the cheek and promised, 'I'll be back to do the chores bright and early, Pa.'

★　★　★

From a wooded slope to the south of the trail, Henry Scranton had watched the exchanges between the parties. When he saw Carty, alone, point his nag in the direction of home and Lucy joining the sheriff headed for town, Scranton reckoned that his luck was in. He chuckled. 'You're kiddin' yourself if you think that Carty gal will sniff near you, Tyrell.' She might have come to him seemingly of her own free will just hours before, but he reckoned that her visit had been prompted by some bust-up between her and her pa, probably about the stranger; women had a thing about the bad ones, he could vouch for that.

He waited until the distance between Carty heading back to his ranch and the others making tracks for town had opened up. Then, evil in his heart, Henry Scranton left cover and tracked Hank Carty. His plan was simple. He'd grab Carty, take him to the old trail and dump him into the ravine, careful to make it look like an accident.

* * *

'Ants in your pants?' Ben Allwood questioned Tod Lacey. 'The way you're jumping about in the saddle.'

Convinced that he had not been mistaken about the watcher, Lacey's unease had increased with every hoof-beat since they had parted company with Hank Carty, who was now riding on his own. Why he should be worried about the man who, if his daughter had not pinned him down, would probably have let him hang to hold on to that daughter he could not say. But he was honest enough to admit to himself that had he been in Carty's boots, he'd also likely have done anything to stop his daughter riding off with a roving man.

While pondering, Barrow caught a glimpse of a rider, easing out of the trees on a wooded slope to the south of the trail and heading in the direction Carty had taken. Alarm bells rang. Hank Carty was all alone and unsuspecting, and would make an easy target. He was about to voice his concerns when he bit his tongue. He'd only panic Lucy, and probably not convince Allwood, who would likely see it as some ruse on his part to slip his guardianship.

So that only left one course of action open to him. He would have to pick his time and make a break for it.

★   ★   ★

Burdened with guilt about the wrong he had done Lacey, and worried anew about losing Lucy to him, Hank Carty's mind was not on the trail ahead, a trail he had ridden a thousand times over and did not need to monitor closely, which allowed him to slip deeper into his preoccupying thoughts.

'Howdy!'

Carty focused on the figure blocking the trail a short distance ahead. He recognized the man as Henry Scranton, a Tyrell hardcase. He let his hand drop closer to his pistol — a wasted action, he reckoned, because he had no doubt that if it came to gunplay he'd be eating dust before he even got near clearing leather.

'Something I can do for you, mister?' he enquired of Scranton.

'Don't think so,' Scranton returned cockily.

'Then if you'll just move aside and let me get by — '

'Can't do that, Carty.'

'Oh?'

Scranton sniggered. 'You see, you're my ticket to easy street.'

★　★　★

'Ahhhhgh!'

'What the hell's wrong?' Allwood asked when Tod Lacey hunched over, clutching his midriff.

'Tod!' Her concern for Lacey's welfare had Lucy Carty sprinting forward, as Lacey would have wished.

'Hold up, Lucy,' the sheriff of Lucky Hollow shouted, too late.

In a flash of movement, Lacey clutched Lucy from her saddle and used her as a shield.

'Damn you, woman!' Allwood bellowed.

Dismayed at Lacey's apparent betrayal, Lucy Carty railed against him: 'You're every bit the snake my pa figured you were.'

'Drop the hardware, Sheriff! Six-gun and rifle.'

'I should've let you hang,' Lucy said.

When Allwood hesitated to do as he had ordered, Lacey said, 'Drop the hardware, or I'll shoot the girl.' Seething, Allwood complied. 'Now back off to the side of the trail and give me a wide berth.'

Grim-faced, Ben Allwood did as requested, promising: 'This isn't the last of this, Lacey, so help me God.'

'Join the sheriff,' Jeff Barrow ordered Lucy. He spurred his horse into a full-blooded gallop, hoping that he was in time to prevent the dark deed he reckoned was being planned for Hank Carty.

* * *

'Ride on, Carty,' Henry Scranton ordered. 'And remember, I've got you covered.'

'Why don't you shoot me down here?' Hank Carty asked, genuinely

190

puzzled, riding up the twisting slope to a trail he knew had been out of favour for an age.

'Could do. And would do, too. But you see, your death must look like one of those darn awful accidents. If I shot you down, what hope d'ya think Tyrell would have of gettin' that fine gal of yours 'tween the sheets. And, if that happened, my ticket to easy street would be up in smoke.'

He grinned, shrewdly reading Carty's thoughts.

'I guess that now you're thinkin' that if you make me shoot you down, you'll save your gal from a cur like Ike Bateman getting his hands on your daughter — '

'Ike Bateman?'

'That's Sam Tyrell's real name, Carty. Now, as I was saying: force me to shoot you down, and I'll settle for what I can get, Carty. And that'll be your gal. I'll use her first like a mangy dog, and then, when I've had my fill of pleasuring, I'll trade her 'cross the border to a whorehouse.'

His laughter mimicked a hyena's cry. 'Ain't much of a choice, is it?'

★ ★ ★

'Barrow!' Sheriff Ben Allwood exclaimed, swinging on board the mare. 'Jeff Barrow,' he told a bemused Lucy Carty. 'JB on his gun stands for Jeff Barrow.'

'What're you going crazy about, Sheriff?' Lucy Carty asked, not much interested, being deep in her despondency at having been deceived by Tod Lacey.

'His name is not Tod Lacey,' Allwood explained. 'And he ain't no saddle tramp neither. Just a man down on his luck, Lucy. I knew I recognized his jib,' he added happily.

'Don't know what you're all so surefire over the moon about,' Lucy said.

'Jeff Barrow was the marshal in a town called Haley's Ridge, which I visited a long time ago when it was raw and rough. Barrow tamed it, and in doing so became the finest lawman in the territory. He made Haley's Ridge the kind of burg that hardcases gave a wide berth to.'

'Marshal?' Lucy yelped delightedly. 'Tod? I mean Jeff?' Then, doubtfully: 'What's he doing as a trail bum, then?'

Ben Allwood told Lucy Carty of the awful happenings in Haley's Ridge, which had made Jeff Barrow take to the life of a trail bum.

Lucy didn't know whether to cry or dance an Irish jig. All she was sure of was that her heart was full of love for Tod Lacey or, as she now knew him to be, Jeff Barrow. 'Poor Jeff,' Lucy wailed.

'A posse ran Bateman's partners to ground and killed them,' Allwood explained. 'But Ike Bateman slipped the noose, and ain't been heard of since.'

'What is it, Sheriff?' Lucy asked, when Ben Allwood frowned thoughtfully, rubbing his chin. 'Word had it that this fella Bateman caught a bullet that creased his left eyebrow, giving an odd angle to it.'

'Sam Tyrell's left eye seems out of kilter with his right one,' Lucy said, now equally thoughtful.

'Yeah,' Allwood said. 'Ain't that a real coincidence!'

'Maybe you should ask Tyrell how he came by that odd-looking left eye of his, Sheriff,' Lucy suggested.

'I aim to, Lucy,' Ben Allwood stated determinedly. 'I just knew Tod, I mean Jeff, was no saddle tramp.' Lucy sighed dreamily. 'But I admit that my belief was pretty shaken just now when he lit out the way he did. If Jeff's not a wanted man, and he's not headed for the border — '

'Then where is he headed, Sheriff?'

Ben Allwood's expression was one of keen concern. 'Your pa, Lucy! He's gone after your pa.'

'Why?' she asked worriedly.

'That I don't know. But I aim to find out.'

15

As Hank Carty neared the ravine on the crumbling outlaw trail, he reckoned that he knew what Scranton's plan for murder was. Folk would ask and ponder about what he had been doing in such a dangerous place, and they might have their suspicions, but nothing would be proved. The bald facts would be that, for some reason, he was on the trail and due to its poor state had fallen into the ravine. As Scranton said, an accident pure and simple.

Now, too late, and worried about Lucy falling into Tyrell's evil clutches, Hank Carty wished he had sold up and moved on when he had had the chance.

'Want I should jump?' he asked bitterly.

'No. The nag goes with you. It'll make it more believable that way.'

'I'll see you in hell!' Carty shouted.

'Probably,' Scranton conceded. 'Now . . .'

He waved Hank Carty to the edge of the ravine with his six-gun.

'Hold it!'

On hearing Jeff Barrow's command, Henry Scranton swung round.

'You got two choices, mister,' Barrow said. 'Go where you were going to send Hank Carty. Or to a noose back in Lucky Hollow.'

'Ain't no choice at all,' Scranton growled.

'Guess not,' Barrow said tonelessly.

'How come you cottoned on to this, mister?'

'Well, I figured with Tyrell wanting Lucy Carty as his wife, it wouldn't do him any good to murder her pa. So it would have to look like an accident. And what better place to have an accident than on a trail that ain't been ridden on in an age, except for the odd fella like me. You had a head start, mister, but a trail bum like me gets to know all the short cuts.'

'Smart fella,' Henry Scranton complimented. 'Pity you ain't as rotten inside as me. We'd have made great pards. What's your name?'

'Jeff Barrow.'

Henry Scranton's eyes popped. 'Barrow? The former marshal of Haley's Ridge?'

'Marshal?' Hank Carty said, eyes popping even wider than Scranton's.

'That's me, Mr Carty,' Jeff Barrow confirmed.

Scranton made to shoot, but he froze as Jeff Barrow's bullet shattered his chest. 'Darn, that's the thing about luck. It runs out when you need it most.' He sat for a moment gripping his saddle horn, before he toppled into the ravine.

'Why didn't you just say who you were?' Carty grumbled. 'Then there'd have been no need for me to lie to my gal!'

'It's only now that I can lay claim to that name again,' Barrow said.

Ben Allwood scrambled up the slope to the trail with Lucy in tow. 'Barrow,' he said. 'I've got real interesting news for you.'

Ike Bateman, alias Sam Tyrell, was pacing back and forth across his den, checking his pocket watch and anxiously awaiting Henry Scranton's return, when he heard his name called out.

'Bateman! Ike Bateman!'

He went to the window and knew instantly the name of the stranger in the yard calling him out, the man whose gait had seemed familiar when he saw him ride away from the Carty place: Jeff Barrow, the former marshal of Haley's Ridge. He was the husband of the woman he'd shot in the back there when he had robbed the bank, the proceeds of which, after he'd lain low in Mexico for a spell, had set him up.

'Step outside, Bateman,' Jeff Barrow shouted. 'Or I'll come in and haul you out to the nearest tree!'

Nervous at first, Ike Bateman's panic soon calmed. He had a passel of hardcases he could call on, so there was nothing to fear. He did as Barrow had asked and stepped outside.

'You loco bastard,' he mocked Barrow. 'You've just walked into the lion's den.'

Bateman looked beyond Jeff Barrow to the men watching. 'String him up, fellas,' he ordered. But no one moved. 'Did you hear what I said?' he roared. 'I said string him up!'

One man stepped forward.

'Ain't goin' to do it, Bateman,' he said. 'Sheriff Allwood's been tellin' us about how you backshot Barrow's woman, and she carryin' an' all?' He pointed over his shoulder at the men assembled behind him. 'We've decided that we don't wanna work for this outfit no more.'

He rejoined the men and they dispersed towards the corral.

The colour drained from Ike Bateman's face. Perspiration oozed from his pores. He looked about like the trapped animal he was.

'No way out, Bateman,' Jeff Barrow said. 'Except over my dead body. Or you can hand yourself over to the sheriff, and you'll most certainly hang.'

Ike Bateman knew he had only one option. He dived for his gun, but was several seconds too late. Barrow had him cold. Bateman fell to his knees, pleading for his life. Lucy came and took Jeff's hand in hers.

'There's been too much killing,' Jeff said, and threw his gun away.

Bateman grabbed his chance. But before he could pull the trigger Ben Allwood cut him down. The riders passed by on their way out, followed by Jeff and Lucy sharing a saddle. Then Hank Carty and Ben Allwood followed.

The only one remaining behind was Ike Bateman, his face in the dust, his blood forming in a pool around him.

★ ★ ★

The next morning Jeff Barrow was a mile outside Lucky Hollow, heading south to the border, when Lucy Carty caught him up.

'Darn, you move quick, Jeff Barrow,'

she said, breathless from her helter-skelter pursuit.

'Didn't figure that there was anything to slow my pace for, Lucy.'

'Will you just hold up for a second!'

Barrow drew rein. 'I'm holding.'

'This ain't easy, you know.'

'What ain't easy?'

'Me having to propose, of course. Figured you weren't going to do it.'

Barrow smiled. 'These days, Lucy,' he wiped trail dust from clothing that had seen better days, 'I ain't the marrying kind.'

'If you'd just hang around, I'm good at persuading.'

'And I ain't none too good at listening. But thanks for the offer.'

'We could have lots of babies.'

'You will, with the right man, Lucy.'

'You are the right man, Jeff Barrow. Knew the second I clapped eyes on you. Pa says, come back, work the ranch with him, and give him grandchildren.'

Barrow smiled. 'A tempting offer that.'

'Then give in to the temptation, Jeff,' Lucy pleaded.

He shook his head. 'So long, Lucy.'

Lucy watched him ride off, her heart going with him every step of the way. 'Goodbye, Jeff,' she wept. 'God bless you.'

★ ★ ★

It was the following autumn when Hank Carty looked up from a chore he was attending to and saw a rider on the ridge overlooking the ranch — a rider whose bearing looked familiar.

'Lucy!' he yelled.

A disconsolate figure came to the kitchen door. 'What's got you so fired up, Pa?'

'He's back,' he said. Lucy Carty followed her father's pointed finger to the rider coming off the ridge. 'Go inside. Take off that apron and put on a gown. And make yourself look pretty.'

Heart beating like a steam hammer, Lucy turned back into the house, but changed her mind. 'No, Pa. If Jeff Barrow's come back for me, he'll want me any way I look.'

She walked out of the yard to meet him.

'You married, Lucy?' he asked, when they met.

'No.'

'Thinking about it?'

'Never stopped.'

'That a fact?'

'That's a fact.'

'How many babies?'

'How many do you want?'

'Ain't rightly decided.'

'Then let's talk about that, Jeff Barrow,' Lucy said.

'Talking's dangerous. Maybe we should find a preacher before we start all this talking?'

'Fine by me, Jeff,' she said.

'Fine by me too, Lucy,' he said.

Hank Carty was a happy man when Jeff Barrow dismounted and danced his daughter about in a merry jig. He crossed the yard, out to the patch behind the house where Martha Carty's grave was.

'Guess we're goin' to have the patter of tiny feet round here, honey,' he said. 'Sure hope you'll like that.'

He took the gentle breeze that blew across his face as a ghostly kiss of Martha's approval.

THE END

We do hope that you have enjoyed reading this large print book.

Did you know that all of our titles are available for purchase?

We publish a wide range of high quality large print books including:
Romances, Mysteries, Classics
General Fiction
Non Fiction and Westerns

Special interest titles available in large print are:
The Little Oxford Dictionary
Music Book, Song Book
Hymn Book, Service Book

Also available from us courtesy of Oxford University Press:
Young Readers' Dictionary
(large print edition)
Young Readers' Thesaurus
(large print edition)

For further information or a free brochure, please contact us at:
Ulverscroft Large Print Books Ltd.,
The Green, Bradgate Road, Anstey,
Leicester, LE7 7FU, England.
Tel: (00 44) **0116 236 4325**
Fax: (00 44) **0116 234 0205**

GUNSLINGER BREED

Corba Sunman

Gunslinger Clint Halloran rides into Plainsville to help his pal Jeff Deacon, hoping to end his friend's troubles. But Deacon is on the point of being lynched, so he fires a shot. Now Halloran has a fight on his hands, a situation complicated by the crooked deputy sheriff, Dan Ramsey, who has his own agenda. Halloran, refusing to give up the fight, vows to keep his gun by his side — right until the final shot is fired.

DEAD END TRAIL

Tyler Hatch

Chet Rand is a decent, law-abiding man, but a forest fire wipes out his horse ranch, leaving him with nothing. However, when he comes across the outlaw Feeney — with a $1,100 reward on his head — it seems like a gift from heaven. Unfortunately, there are many shady characters in pursuit of the $12,000 Feeney has stolen — a more pressing matter than the bounty itself. So it's inevitable that when guns are drawn, blood will flow and men will die . . .

DUEL AT DEL NORTE

Ethan Flagg

Russ Wikeley settles in Del Norte, South Dakota, and after foiling a bank robbery he's persuaded to stand for sheriff in the town's elections. However, Diamond Jim Stoner, a gang boss, wants his own man to become sheriff and attempts to undermine Wikeley. When his plan backfires, he tries to frame his adversary for robbery and murder. Both men are determined . . . only one can be the victor in the final duel on the streets of Del Norte.

THE KILLING KIND

Lance Howard

Jim Bartlett thought he could put his past behind him and forge a new life in Texas, as a small ranch owner — but he was wrong . . . dead wrong. Someone from his past has followed him and is systematically trying to destroy his new life, piece by piece. With his friends and the woman he loves being threatened by a man who knows no remorse, Jim struggles desperately — not only to escape his past — but also to hold onto his life . . .

RAKING HELL

Lee Clinton

A body is wrapped in a bloodstained horse-blanket. A farmer admits to the gruesome crime, but with good reason. So will the sheriff arrest or protect the guilty man when eight men come looking to settle the score? After all, the sheriff has taken an oath to protect the town . . . This story of judgement, consequence and the promise of retribution, tells of one man — Sheriff Will Price — who is prepared to go raking hell to fulfil his pledge . . .